All hail the new Eric Ambler!

"Eric Ambler is one of the best mystery writers around; this is his best spying spoof."
—Newsday

"The old master is back, with a clever, witty, altogether different spy story."
—Publishers' Weekly

"His wit is triple sec."
—Playboy

"It comes just in time to lend new life to a genre we all love and lately despaired of."
—Book World

"THE INTERCOM CONSPIRACY has all the ingredients of the first-class spy thriller—good writing, believable people, suspense!"
—Book-of-the-Month Club News

THE INTERCOM CONSPIRACY begins when two top-level agents decide it's time to come in from the cold and launch an international blackmail plot destined to blow every NATO and Warsaw Pact secret sky high.

Bantam Books by Eric Ambler

The Intercom Conspiracy

Eric Ambler

BANTAM BOOKS
TORONTO · NEW YORK · LONDON

A NATIONAL GENERAL COMPANY

This low-priced Bantam Book
has been completely reset in a type face
designed for easy reading, and was printed
from new plates. It contains the complete
text of the original hard-cover edition.
NOT ONE WORD HAS BEEN OMITTED.

THE INTERCOM CONSPIRACY

A Bantam Book / published by arrangement with
Atheneum Publishers

PRINTING HISTORY
Antheneum edition published December 1969
Bantam edition published December 1970

Bantam Books are published by Bantam Books, Inc., a National
General company. Its trade-mark, consisting of the words "Bantam
Books" and the portrayal of a bantam, is registered in the United
States Patent Office and in other countries. Marca Registrada.
Bantam Books, Inc., 666 Fifth Avenue, New York, N.Y. 10019.

PRINTED IN THE UNITED STATES OF AMERICA

CONTENTS

Foreword

It was on May 31 of last year, at Geneva's Cointrin airport, that the man who called himself Charles Latimer disappeared. All efforts to trace him have so far failed.

Through a combination of circumstances the disappearance went unreported for two weeks.

Much has been made of this long delay and of the difficulties it is said to have created for the police and security authorities concerned. In fact it was of little importance. All the evidence we now have suggests that a delay of a single day would have had the same effect. Within a few hours of his leaving the airport Charles Latimer became permanently untraceable.

Though his home was in Majorca, he had spent most of the three months prior to his disappearance in Switzerland. He had gone there to do research for a book commissioned by his American publisher and to work on the manuscript of it. To assist him in Geneva he had employed a secretary, Mlle Deladoey.

It was she who eventually sounded the alarm.

That she did not do so earlier is understandable. Latimer had told her that he was going to Evere in Belgium to interview a senior officer on the staff of NATO. There was nothing remarkable about that. It was not the first trip he had taken from his Geneva base in connection with the book he was writing; he had previously interviewed persons in Munich, Bonn, Bâle, Bern and Luxembourg. Evere is near Brussels. Mlle Deladoey made the airline and Brussels hotel reservations through a travel agency.

He did not tell her how long he expected to be gone and she did not ask him. Nor did anyone else. He always retained his Geneva hotel room when he went on these trips and left most of his luggage there. On this occasion he took only a single piece with him. Mlle Deladoey assumed that he would be away for no more than two or three days. The amount of retyping work he had given her to do in his absence supported that assumption.

When eight days had elapsed without word from him, she became sufficiently uneasy to send a telegram to Brussels asking when he would be back. She received no reply. Six more days passed. By then her concern had been deepened by the fact that she was owed two weeks' wages. She sought the advice of the senior receptionist at Latimer's Geneva hotel.

He shared her concern, though for different reasons. He was the cashier as well as the receptionist and he judged guests who lived for extended periods in the hotel by the way they paid their weekly bills. Latimer had always paid promptly, by Crédit Suisse cheque, on the same day that the bill was presented. It was, the cashier thought, quite out of character for so punctilious a man to behave with such lack of consideration. Only illness or accident could explain it, and, of the two, illness seemed the more likely; Latimer was not a young man. After consulting the manager, the cashier authorised Mlle Deladoey to put in a telephone call to Brussels.

It took only a few minutes to discover that Latimer was not, and had not been, staying at the Brussels hotel.

Thinking that there might have been some mistake over the name of the hotel, she checked with the travel agency. She was told that there had been no mistake. Persisting in her inquiries, she now found that Latimer had not after all taken the Sabena airline flight to Brussels on which he had been booked. His name had been on the passenger list, but he had not shown up for the flight. Had he perhaps taken a later flight on Sabena or another airline? Or to some destination other than Brussels? Those questions took some hours to answer, but the answers when they came were all negative.

She told the cashier. He again consulted the manager. On the morning of the fifteenth day after the disappearance the police were informed of the situation.

In the canton of Geneva the police procedure for dealing with missing-person reports is comprehensive and thorough. A form of particulars is filled out, hospitals and morgues are checked, relatives are interviewed, teletype reports go out to adjacent police areas and other cantonal police departments, inquiries are made at the place where the missing person was last seen, and, if the person is a foreigner, the appropriate consulate is informed.

In Latimer's case there were no relatives immediately available for interview. He was unmarried and his only surviving blood relative, an elder brother, proved to be on a cruise ship somewhere in the Caribbean. However, once it was established that the last place at which he had been seen was the airport, a number of persons there were questioned. As a result, the press picked up the story almost immediately.

Charles Latimer Lewison described himself in *Who's Who* as an historian; and an historian he undoubtedly was. He had written books about the Hanseatic League, about the growth of banking in the seventeenth century and about the Gotha Programme of 1875, for example. He had been a university lecturer in England. He was the author of a biography of the eighteenth-century economist John Law considered by some to be the best work on that subject. Yet his reputation, outside a small segment of the academic world, rested on none of those achievements; it rested on the detective stories he wrote under the pseudonym of Charles Latimer. There were over twenty of these, and at least three —*A Bloody Shovel, Murder's Arms* and *No Doornail This*—had come to be regarded as classics in the genre. His work as an historian could only be read in English and had a limited appeal. His detective stories had been translated into many languages and had a worldwide appeal. They made not only his reputation as an entertainer but also the income on which he lived so comfortably in Majorca. When he disappeared they also made him news. As every reporter and most editorial writers hastened to point out, his disappearance was as mysterious and bizarre as one of his own novels.

Had he disappeared intentionally? If so, why and how?

Had he been abducted? If so, how and why?

Was he alive or dead?

Dead or alive, *where* was he?

Those were the questions the newspapers asked. Those, too, were the questions the police asked.

Some answers were forthcoming; but, since they only raised more questions, they gave little satisfaction.

It was, for instance, established that Latimer had had no appointment to interview a senior NATO officer in Evere. He had, then, lied to Mlle Deladoey; he had not wanted her to know where he was really going.

Why not? What was it that had to be kept so secret from a temporary secretary? What would her knowledge of his true destination have told her? And why, if he had hoped to keep his mysterious journey secret, had he not returned as unobtrusively as he had departed? There was every indication that he had intended to return. What could have happened to make him change his plans? Had his plans perhaps been changed for him?

It was Mlle Deladoey herself, wearied by hours of police interrogation, who suggested that the answers might possibly be found in the unfinished book the missing man had been writing. Why, she asked, did they not read the typed manuscript which was on his desk at the hotel?

The police were at first inclined to dismiss the suggestion. Not unnaturally, they assumed that the work in question was a detective story. When they learned that it was not, however, and had been persuaded to read it, they reacted sharply. Mlle Deladoey was subjected to further and more searching interrogations and not only by the police; representatives of the Swiss federal security service had moved in by then. On June 25, ten days after the disappearance had been reported, she was visited by a security official who wanted to know if she had any more copies of the Latimer manuscript in her possession. She gave him the two carbons she had made and he gave her a receipt for them.

She did not ask why he wanted the copies. If she had done so, she would have been told that the manuscript had been given a security classification and that orders had been issued to impound all copies of the document. As it was, she assumed that they wanted additional copies because it had been found inconvenient to have only one.

It did not occur to her, therefore, to mention the draft manuscripts that existed. Nor did she mention the box of tape recordings in her stationery drawer. Those things, after all, were Mr. Latimer's property.

Or were they now, perhaps, *her* property?

Later that day she wrote to Latimer's publishers telling them about the tapes and about the draft manuscripts in her and Mr. Theodore Carter's possession. She also informed them that there were now three weeks' wages due to her.

It is possible, I think, that she had an idea that possession of the tape recordings placed her in some sort of bargaining position. If so, she was very soon disabused of the notion. By that time the publishers had established direct contact with Theodore Carter. As Mr. Carter had been a party to Latimer's contract with them for the book, he was the logical person for them to turn to. Along with her three weeks' wages Mlle Deladoey doubtless received a brief lecture on the laws of copyright.

Publication of the Latimer manuscript, unedited and unabridged, was at first strongly opposed by Mr. Carter.

It is impossible not to sympathise with his objections. Charles Latimer sometimes gave his rather malicious sense of humour too free a rein, and his deliberate inclusion, verbatim in the original text, of many of Mr. Carter's off-the-record asides and comments, as well as personal communications not intended for publication, is hard to defend. Clearly, Latimer had been amusing himself privately at Mr. Carter's expense.

Mr. Carter's decision to withdraw his objections to the inclusion of the offending passages is wholly to his credit. An appeal was made to his professional judgment and he responded to it in a thoroughly professional way. The argument upon which the appeal was based was, I feel, a compelling one.

The two-part manuscript which the police and the security people read, and promptly classified, was a second draft. The manuscript which Mlle Deladoey so reluctantly surrendered was a very rough first draft. It was organised in chapters, but very unevenly. A few chapters, the "narrative reconstructions" principally, were fairly well polished; the rest were assemblages of material—letters, transcribed tape recordings, interviews and statements—strung together in chronological order and extensively blue-pencilled by Latimer. It was by noting the passages that Latimer, for his own private security reasons, had deleted from the first draft that Mr. Carter obtained in the end the evidence needed, not only to solve the mystery of the disappearance but also to tell the rest of the story.

That first draft, then, was in a sense definitive.

In withdrawing his objections, Mr. Carter made only one condition. Certain names, he said, must be changed, "to protect the guilty."

Two such changes have been made.

The rest is left, unedited, to speak for itself.

ERIC AMBLER

Part One

The Consortium

ONE

FROM THEODORE CARTER
(transcribed dictation tape)

All right, Nicole, my dear, you've got Mr. Latimer's letter. Or docs he call himself Lewison? Well, whichever it is, this is what I want to say to him.

Dear Mr. Whatsit,

I have received your letter of whatever the date is, and duly noted the contents. You ask if I would be so "kind" as to cooperate with you in preparing for publication in book form a full and authentic account of the "so-called" *Intercom* affair. Then, after a lot more guff, you hint at the possibility that, if I'm very good, there may be a little something in it later for me. An honorarium you call it.

Well, that's nice. Would I be right in suspecting that you had a lawyer draft that letter for you? It smelt like it. I particularly like the word "kind."

Mr. Thing, let's cut the cackle, shall we?

I can quite well see that you need my cooperation. As I was and am the worst-hit casualty of the *Intercom* affair (why "so-called"—how else would you refer to it?), and as I was the person at the receiving end of all the rough stuff, and as I am the only protagonist still breathing who is able and willing to talk for the record, it's pretty clear, I'd say, that without my cooperation you haven't a hope in hell.

You talk about a *full and authentic* account. Don't kid yourself, Mr. Thing. Don't think you can get *that* by browsing through the news-magazine files and having cozy chats with the Swiss security boys. You can't. I still have a lot of inside stuff that the bogeymen persuaded me to keep under my hat, and that has not *so far* been published. You don't know the half of it. There may even be some things that I *still* can't talk about. But, where info about the *Intercom* affair is concerned, I am, you'd better face it, the one and only horse's mouth.

That does not mean, Mr. Whatsit, that I am prepared to make a horse's arse out of myself.

Why the hell should *I* be kind?

You may be a distinguished writer of *romans policiers,* but has it escaped your notice that I am an experienced editor, wire-service reporter and re-write man? Don't let the fact that I worked for *Intercom* fool you or influence your thinking. It didn't influence the thinking of the Italian publisher who approached me with the proposition that *I* should write a full and authentic account of the affair for book publication. Nor did it influence the thinking of the American magazine editor who made a special trip from Paris to suggest that I do a three-part piece on the affair for them.

Why didn't I accept those offers? Because they weren't good enough, that's why. What the Italian was offering for world rights wouldn't have kept me in tranquilizers while I was bashing it out. What the Americans had in mind was that I should spill the beans to one of their tame "as-told-to" boys for a thousand bucks and my name on the cover page. I soon told them where they could shove *that* one.

I am not desperate, Mr. Thing, and I am not interested in crap about possible honoraria. If you want cooperation from me, *you're* the one who's going to have to be kind.

4

What *I* mean by kind is this.

We stop talking about cooperation—the word is collaboration. We stop talking about honoraria—the terms are 50 per cent of the proceeds, *all* the proceeds.

Take it or leave it.

My guess is you'll have to take it, because if you don't, I'm not going to talk; and if I don't talk, your account is going to be about as full and authentic as your maiden aunt's codpiece. What's more —and I hope you'll take this in good part, Mr. Thing, because, though I don't yet know you personally, I'm hoping that ours can be a beautiful friendship—I know enough about the laws of libel, copyright, misrepresentation and invasion of privacy, here and elsewhere, to be really troublesome if my name is taken in vain. That isn't a threat, but it could be a promise.

So let's assume that we're going to be collaborators. You say that you plan to make this, to use your own mellifluous prose—*get this quote right, Nicole* —"a chronological account composed partly of transcribed and edited tape recordings of statements by important witnesses willing to be identified, and partly of narrative reconstructions based on evidence obtained from involved persons and others who for various reasons must remain anonymous." In other words, a scissors-and-paste job.

Well, I have a couple of things to say about that.

As you have probably already found, the only *important* witness willing to be identified is me. That means that I'm going to be doing quite a lot of the work—and explains, incidentally, why I'm asking for half the proceeds. *But,* Mr. Thing, while I may be willing to stand up and be counted, I am definitely *not* willing to be edited. You'd better understand that now. Nothing I say or write is going to be abridged, abbreviated, cut, rearranged, reorganised, modified or "improved" by you or anyone else. I'm not asking that my name go up in lights as collaborator and I'm not interested in narrative reconstructions (Christ, what a phrase!) or any arrangements you may make with other witnesses, if any. What I am insisting on is that everything *I* say or write goes in *exactly* as is, without any change or distortion, and that it is properly credited to me: From Theodore Carter.

Get me another drink, will you, love? There should be a fresh bottle in the stair cupboard.
Sorry, Nicole. Forgot to switch off. Val's here.

So there it is, Mr. Whatsit. As soon as I get a letter from you confirming your acceptance of the terms and conditions I have outlined here, plus a copy of your contract with the commissioning publisher, plus a cheque for 50 per cent of the advance (dollars or Swiss francs, either will do), we're in business. The publisher can countersign our letter agreement.

Oh, one more thing. Under no circumstances, Mr. Whatsit, am I prepared to have anything to do, directly or indirectly, with any of those persons you mention who can't or won't be identified. That department's all yours. Chicken? You bet I am. I've had enough of those buggers to last me a lifetime. And if you'll take a tip from me, you'll meet them only in broad daylight and in public places with plenty of other people around and a policeman within sight. You'll have trouble enough with those "narrative reconstructions." You don't want to end up needing a reconstruction job on yourself, too.

Nicole, my dear, scrub the last paragraph. I don't want him getting cold feet. Then clean it up a bit, end yours sincerely and do an extra carbon. No, wait. Better do a draft for me to see first. After all, this is business.

FROM CHARLES LATIMER

Dear Mr. Carter,

Thank you for your letter. I found it most entertaining. I do hope, however, that I am not expected to take all the proposals you make in it seriously.

You appear to favour the forthright, no-nonsense method of doing business. I say "appear to" because, of course, exhortations to face the facts and cut the cackle are often the reverse of what they seem; the most devious men commonly profess simplicity. However, I will take you at what appears to be your word and speak plainly.

There is always a tendency among those who have survived a harrowing experience to exaggerate the danger they were in and to assume that they alone are qualified to speak about it. As an experienced journalist you should be aware of that tendency and so be capable of observing it in yourself.

You say that you were the worst-hit casualty of the *Intercom* affair and are the only surviving protagonist. My dear Mr. Carter, you were a minor casualty and never a protagonist. You just looked like those things, because you were standing on that small piece of the iceberg that showed above the surface. You don't really know what hit you; you only *think* you know. There are two ways of describing your part in the affair—as that of an innocent bystander caught in a bank hold-up, or as the victim of a practical joke perpetrated by strangers.

You don't understand what I am now talking about, do you? Quite so. Your view of what you call the *Intercom* affair is a very restricted one. All you know is what happened to you. You don't know why or exactly how it happened. I do know *why,* and I am now beginning, because I am taking the necessary trouble and a certain amount of risk, to discover *how*. There is more than one horse's mouth, Mr. Carter.

It does not surprise me in the least to hear that the offers you have received for your story have been disappointing. What does surprise me is that at this late stage you have received any offers at all. That is why I thought that my suggestion of a fee (yes, I am afraid that "honorarium" was lawyer's language) in return for your cooperation might be acceptable. My offer is still open. If you saw your way to accepting it, I could probably see my way to accepting by letter agreement the conditions you make about acknowledgment and editing.

Don't misunderstand me, please. In stressing the narrowness of your view I am not trying to belittle your position. A contribution from you in statement form would be valuable. It would not, however, be indispensable. You see, I already know much more about the *Intercom* affair than you do.

That I got to know the "why" part of it by accident rather than by design, I freely admit. That is how I first became interested in the affair. Through a friend in the country where I spend the autumn of my days I became acquainted with the man I am calling "Colonel Jost" in the book. The Colonel is in retirement now and already a little bored by it. He likes company and he likes to talk. He especially liked talking to me because I have written some books he has enjoyed. Thrillers and detective stories are his favourite reading; they make him laugh.

I am sorry that you dislike the phrase "narrative reconstruction," but perhaps you won't object to reading one. I wrote it after listening to Colonel Jost talk. It is entitled "A Game for Two Players" and may help explain why certain things happened to you.

It may even persuade you to accept my offer after all.

Yours sincerely,
CHARLES LATIMER

TWO

A GAME FOR TWO PLAYERS

The steamer from Evian on the French side of the lake had made its stop at Territet. Now it came into sight again and turned to head for the pier on which Colonel Jost stood waiting.

He looked down at the water. He remembers that there was a cold breeze blowing along the lake that day and that waves were breaking over the boulders along the shore. The sight did not interest him in the least. He came from a country with a coastline open to North Sea gales, and these waves, he says, reminded him of slopping bath water; but he kept his eyes on them just the same. It was better than staring expectantly at the approaching steamer, and better than appearing to examine, even idly, the other persons waiting beside him on the pier. There were five of them: two women with bulging string bags, a seedy man carrying an imitation-leather sample case, and a pair of out-of-season German tourists, husband and wife. All probably harmless, he thought, but you could never be certain; and if you appeared not to notice people, there was less chance of their noticing and remembering you. He kept staring at the waves until the steamer came alongside.

Paddle wheels churned, mooring lines were passed, the gangway was pushed out. Four persons

9

came ashore. The waiting passengers walked on board.

Jost went last and saw his friend Brand almost immediately.

Brand was sitting in the saloon, on the starboard side by one of the windows.

Neither man gave any sign of recognition. Jost walked up the companionway, turning up the fur collar of his coat as he went, and took a seat on the upper deck.

His expression of bored indifference to his surroundings remained, but for several seconds he had had to make a conscious effort to preserve it. He had had a shock.

It had been over six months since he had seen Brand, and in that time his friend's appearance had changed remarkably. Brand had always been pale; that kind of pale, slightly sallow complexion is not uncommon among Scandinavians. But always before it had been a healthy pallor; there had been blood beneath the skin. Now, the face was pinched and grey and the life seemed to have gone out of it. Suddenly, Brand looked old and either very sick or very frightened.

The last thought made Jost's muscles tighten for a moment. He forced himself to relax. Brand had requested this meeting and said that the need for it was urgent. With secret meetings of this kind there was always an element of risk to be accepted. If on this occasion the risks were for some reason to be greater than usual, Brand's message would surely have said so. It had not said so. Therefore his appearance must be due to illness. Nothing in the message about that either; but then the method of private communication which they employed had not been designed to convey information about personal matters.

He remembered the night they had worked out the method, on the garden terrace of a hotel near Strasbourg.

A French ten-franc note has on its face side four groups of figures. There is the date of issue and a printing-batch number. Then there are two serial numbers, one of five figures in the lower left-hand corner and one of ten figures in the centre below the words *Banque de France*. In all, there are at least twenty-five digits on every note, and no two of the notes are exactly alike. It had been Brand's idea to use these notes as "one-time" cypher pads. Jost himself had devised the matrix. The method was crude, no doubt, but it worked and was as safe as such things could be: a ten-franc note in one airmail envelope, the encyphered message in another. The limitation was that you could only send short, simple messages.

The message which had brought him there had been short and simple:

> URGENT MEET PROPOSE COVER MI-
> LAN THEN VISIT GODCHILD TWEN-
> TIETH PM EVIAN STEAMER AFTER
> VEVEY CONFIRM.

Well, perhaps it was not really simple. A good deal of thought had gone into its composition.

Even in those parts of the world where international travel is easy and commonplace, there are some persons—presidents, kings, prime ministers and known criminals, for example—who can never, as ordinary men can, move freely from country to country, meeting whom they please where they choose, without their comings and goings being more than casually supervised.

Directors of government secret intelligence services are among these inhibited few.

In their own countries they are able to shroud their movements in secrecy and generally prefer to do so; but the moment they plan to go abroad, questions will be asked, and not only by their subordinates and those to whom they are technically responsible. Protocol, and sometimes prudence, demands that the foreign colleagues into whose territories they are moving be informed of their movements and of the reasons for them. Since such travellers must always expect to be under some sort of surveillance—at best benevolent and protective, but invariably careful and inquisitive—the reasons they give, whether true or false, must never be less than convincing.

A director of a secret intelligence service himself, with personal experience of the problem, Colonel Brand had thoughtfully suggested a good cover story for his friend's use on this occasion. The suggestion was contained in the message references to Milan and visiting a godchild.

In Milan during the week immediately prior to the date of the proposed meeting, an international electronics-industry fair would be in progress. New miniaturized sensing and detection devices would be shown, as well as the latest telecommunications equipment. Brand had guessed, correctly, that Jost would be sending a man from his technical section to Milan to report on the new developments. He had also guessed, again correctly, that a decision by Jost to go to Milan himself with the technician would cause no surprise. The decision would be in character; Colonel Jost's interest in technical development was well known.

However, Colonel Brand could not go to Milan for the same reason; for him that would have been out of character. So the meeting would have to be elsewhere.

In addition to the cypher messages they exchanged, they took care to keep up an ordinary, quite innocent private correspondence. Jost, a childless widower, had complained in one of his recent letters that a niece of whom he was fond, and to whom he was godfather, had been sent by her parents to an English school near Montreux in Switzerland. Brand had remembered. What could be more natural than that Jost, on his way back from Milan, should break his journey at Montreux and visit his godchild?

Brand had always been clever with cover stories, Jost reflected. Presumably he had cooked up something equally ingenious to get himself to Evian. It would be amusing to hear.

Well, he would hear soon. They were past the Ile de Salagnon now and heading across the lake towards Vevey.

After Vevey, Brand had said.

They had been friends for fifteen years then—since, in fact, the year of their appointments to the posts they still held.

They had been introduced, under circumstances humiliating to both of them, at a NATO base in France. It had been the humiliation, petty and even laughable when they looked back on it but infuriating at the time, that had first drawn them together.

The title of Brand's post was Director of Security and Intelligence, that of Jost's Director of Defence Intelligence. In effect, the jobs they did for their respective governments were the same; they were opposite numbers. They had other things in common. Both had fought with bravery and distinction in resistance movements when their small countries had been under German occupation. Both had been leaders and organisers, loyal to their governments in exile and, as professional soldiers from "good" families, politically of the right. They had survived the occupation because they were hard, self-reliant and resourceful men, because they had despised heroics and action for action's sake and because they had learned early enough to disobey orders from remote commanders when they knew those orders to be unrealistic or ill-advised. Both had developed the special skills needed for the successful conduct of clandestine operations. As staff officers in the immediate postwar years, their knowledge, experience and natural aptitudes were found to be of the kind needed in intelligence work and they became specialists in it. When the growth of the North Atlantic Treaty Organisation made the creation of their posts necessary, they were the men considered best qualified to fill them. They had no predecessors and were hampered by no precedents. They were from the first very much their own masters.

On their appointment they automatically became full members of a standing joint intelligence committee of NATO on which their countries had been temporarily represented by military attachés. At that time the quarterly three-day meetings of the committee were held at a U.S. Army base twenty kilometers outside Paris. Security arrangements on these top-secret occasions were handled by the Americans.

For the first of these meetings that they attended, Jost and Brand were accommodated in their respective Paris embassies. Both had already received the NATO top-secret security clearance known as Cosmic.* However, since they were new to the committee, it had been necessary for their embassies to obtain from the Americans the special maximum-security passes that would be needed to gain admittance, first to the base and then to the heavily guarded conference area within the base perimeter. These passes were delivered to them personally at their embassies by an American liaison officer.

At eight-thirty on the morning of the first day, Jost and Brand were picked up separately at their embassies by U.S. Army staff cars and driven out to the base. Both were in uniform. They arrived within two minutes of each other at about nine-fifteen. By nine-thirty both were under arrest, or at

---

*A mnemonic for Coordination of Security Measures in International Command.

any rate under armed guard in a guardroom, and being interrogated by an American military-police lieutenant who accused them in highly offensive terms of being newspaper reporters.

It seemed that the lieutenant had recently had an unfortunate experience with some too-enterprising foreign reporters, an experience which had resulted in his being reprimanded by his commanding officer. But he had learned his lesson. Now, he said, he could smell a newsman a mile off. He used a great many four-letter words in expressing his opinion of the two bewildered colonels, in shouting down their protests and in describing what he intended with his own hands to do to them. Nearly ten minutes passed before a captain from the security section arrived to investigate.

The captain was in private life a trained police officer. He silenced the impassioned lieutenant, asked sensible questions and received sensible replies. The nature of the misunderstanding now became apparent. The special passes which had been issued to Jost and Brand were of a type which had been withdrawn a month previously. It was obvious, the captain said, that there had been a foul-up.

Obvious it may have been, but two hours elapsed before the mistake could be corrected. The identification papers the two men carried had no validity in that maximum-security area. Their fingerprints had to be taken, records had to be fetched for purposes of comparison and persons summoned to double-check their identities. They were, of course, late at the committee meeting, where, since the current chairman had not been told about the cause of the delay, they had a cool reception.

During the luncheon break, however, there were explanations and an American major from the security section introduced himself to the two. He did not grovel and he did not invent excuses. He did admit, without equivocation, that the mistake had been due to carelessness in his office and he confirmed that their embassies had been in no way responsible. He apologised unreservedly for the embarrassment and inconvenience the mistake had caused.

His style was engaging and they were reasonable men. Foul-ups, Jost said amiably, were not unknown where he came from, and Brand congratulated the major on his captain, whose courtesy and good sense that morning had eased a trying situation.

If the matter had been allowed to rest there, with an apology unreservedly given and as unreservedly accepted, it is probable that the relationship between Jost and Brand would not have developed quite as it did. The private joke might still have been born, but it would have been short-lived and would have remained *only* a joke.

As it was, the major's superior officer decided that it would be a wise move on his part to apologise personally to these two foreigners. "After all," he pointed out to the major, "they're cloak-and-dagger boys. That means they're creeps. They may act like all is forgiven and forgotten, but did they actually state that they're not going to put in formal complaints? No. I'm not taking any chances. I'll handle them myself." At the end of the day's session he sent a message asking if they would mind stopping by at his office to receive and sign for the new passes that had been prepared for them.

He was a full colonel with two rows of medal ribbons of the kind commonly referred to in the U.S. Army at that time as "spinach." After the business of the new passes had been disposed of, he produced a bottle of whisky and offered them a drink. They accepted. He then moved on to his apology, which began with a brief but confusing description of the pass-issuing procedure and ended with a long, rambling account of the security problems he faced there and of the difficult, responsible, thankless task he had. By the time he had finished, he had not only made it plain that he regarded him-

16

self as the real victim of the foul-up, but had also conveyed the impression that, in his view, they had brought most of the indignities to which they had been subjected that morning on themselves.

"Don't get me wrong," he said with a friendly smile, "but I'm told that it was the strange uniforms that made the sergeant on the outer gate double-check those passes. I don't say that you'd have gotten away with it if he hadn't double-checked—there'd be some heads rolling around here if you had, believe you me—but that's why you had those redneck MPs on your backs first instead of my boys."

"Surely," said Jost as calmly as he could, "our attachés have been attending these meetings in uniform."

"Sure they have. But your attaché is a navy man, and yours—" he looked at Brand—"who has PX privileges here, wears American olive drab. Sure he has his own badges and flashes, but unless you're real close to him he looks strictly GI."

"The appearance of our uniforms is perhaps better known in combat areas," said Brand coldly.

Their host was not put out. "I've no doubt it is, Colonel. As I say, don't get me wrong. We do have a problem here with all these foreign uniforms. We know it and we're trying to lick it. You've seen the NATO wall charts we've put up—uniforms, badges, flashes, flags, the lot. But it's tough. We had a guy here last month in the goddamndest fancy dress you ever saw. He could have been anything—Peruvian field marshal, doorman at a new clip joint, you name it. In fact, he was an Italian captain in some crack outfit of theirs. It's a problem, all right. But I'll tell you this. It's a problem you gentlemen won't have to worry about again. Now, let's freshen up those drinks."

They got away as soon as they could and decided to share a staff car back to Paris.

In the car they nursed their anger in silence for a while. Then Jost cleared his throat.

"The denial that affirms," he said.

Brand stared at him.

Jost cleared his throat again. " 'I would never for a moment suggest that Mr. X is a liar and a thief, *but* . . .' " He pursed his lips distastefully. "I think that 'don't get me wrong, *but*' is a gambit of the same kind. In effect it says, 'What I am going to say will undoubtedly offend you, but, as I have denied in advance that I mean to give offence, you have no right to complain.' All the same, I *do* complain."

Brand smiled. "Then you won't get *me* wrong if I say that I hope that man is still wondering whether he persuaded us to keep our mouths shut. I would like to think of him troubled by doubts."

"So would I. Doubts at the very least." Jost glanced at the American driver in front of them and then went on in French. "Do you intend to lodge a protest?"

"I had decided not to—that is, if you were in agreement with me. Now I am undecided. What is your view?"

Jost thought for a moment. They were both speaking French now.

"I share your disgust and annoyance," Jost said, "and I think that protests would be justified. Whether or not they would serve any useful purpose is another matter. I am inclined, reluctantly, to think that they would not. Besides, one does not want to start out by being labelled difficult."

There was a pause before Brand replied. "I agree," he said. "I shall make a report to my ambassador, of course, but will ask that no action be taken. However," he went on grimly, "I will certainly see that in future our military attaché does *not* wear uniforms obtained cheaply from the American PX. This place has obviously demoralised him."

Jost sighed. "It is all very regrettable. Last week

I was briefed by our army commander. Officials from the defence and foreign ministries attended. The man from the foreign ministry saw fit to warn me of a tendency on the part of some allied representatives here to harbour anti-American sentiments and even sometimes to express them." He gave Brand a sidelong look. "He called anti-Americanism a vice of the most corrupting kind and the one in which we could least afford to indulge, as it was rooted in envy."

"That has an Old Testament ring."

"Our civil officials take themselves seriously. At the time I was offended that such a warning should have been thought necessary, even by that old fool. I didn't know then how soon I would be tempted."

"But *are* we tempted?" Brand shrugged. "You know as well as I do that our friend with the whisky bottle is merely a time-serving buffoon of a type you will find in every army. If the security arrangements had been in other hands, he might have been French or British and, though possibly in different ways, just as offensive. It is not being anti-American to dislike that man."

"And *you* know," Jost retorted, "that that is no argument in our situation. It is the Americans who count now in the West, because only they have the real power and the will to exercise it. Whether *they* like or dislike *us* does not matter—they will value us according to our usefulness within the alliance and our readiness to comply with their wishes. What does matter is that we do not, on that account, permit ourselves to dislike and resent them—*any* of them, for *any* reason, good or bad. Such dislikes or resentments are not in our interest." He paused, then added blandly: "I am again quoting, of course, from my official instructions."

"So I gathered," Brand replied dryly. "I, too, have instructions from my government in which I do not wholly believe."

They eyed each other for a moment and then

smiled. The first step in their mutual understanding had been reached. They suddenly felt at ease with each other.

"So," said Jost, "since such instructions, wholly believed in or not, must still be resolutely obeyed, let us forget the man with the whisky and remember only that good captain and his admirable major."

Brand nodded. "Yes, indeed, let us do that. But—" a faraway look came into his eyes— "don't get me wrong if I remind you of the lieutenant of military police who first interrogated us this morning. Did you not find him specially interesting?"

"Because his first thought was that we must be newspaper reporters in disguise?"

"Yes, and because he appeared to be far more disturbed by that possibility than the possibility of our being enemy agents. That thought did not seem even to enter his head."

"He has had a bad experience with reporters, remember, and no experience at all, probably, with enemy agents."

"Perhaps not. But I prefer a different explanation. I like to think of that man as an instinctive realist."

Jost glanced at his companion warily. "You will have to explain that, I'm afraid."

They were in the city now and the passing street lights flickered on their faces. Brand was smiling.

"A realist in this context," he said, "being one who assumes that most of the secrets we guard so jealously are already well known to the other side, and that most of the secrets the other side guards are already well known to us. One who also understands, however, that the conventions must be observed and the pretences maintained, that outsiders may not look in on our foolishness and that both sides have a common enemy—the small boy who saw that the emperor was naked."

"Dangerous talk, Colonel!"

They began to laugh. Then Jost glanced out of the window and saw that they were nearing their destination. "I take it that you will be dining with your ambassador tonight," he said.

"I'm afraid so. And you with yours?"

"Yes. Perhaps tomorrow evening we could continue these useful bilateral discussions."

"The same thought was in my own mind."

And so the friendship began.

Directors of intelligence services with secret budgets at their disposal and the ability, sometimes the obligation, to put expediency before strict legality tend to become back-room potentates. It is in the nature of their occupation that they should. As long as they and their subordinates avoid committing blunders too gross to be hidden, they are immune from public criticism. The secrecy fetish and a general acceptance of the "need-to-know" principle are very powerful defences. When such defences are reinforced, as they so often are, by politic murmurs of "don't-want-to-know" from nominal superiors, the men behind them are secure even from attacks launched by hostile factions within the establishments they serve. They acquire more authority than their responsibilities warrant. They are accountable virtually to no one; and the longer they remain in their posts the stronger they become. Inevitably they also tend to become arrogant. The arrogance will generally be concealed, of course, behind well-composed masks of professional objectivity and reserve, and the quality of it will vary; but it will be there. How it is expressed will depend on the character of the man concerned, on his hopes, conceits and circumstances, on the political environment in which he works, and on time and chance. There have been directors who have found it amusing to lend support to leaders they despise, as well as those who have followed their consciences when it would have been safer and more profitable to ignore them. There have been directors who became kingmakers, who have subverted the governments they were pledged to serve and helped plan the coups which brought them down. There have been those who have seized power for themselves, and those who have preferred to act as the *éminences grises* of puppet rulers. And there have been those whose arrogance has expressed itself in more eccentric, less familiar, ways.

Jost and Brand came to power in the early nineteen-fifties and established themselves in the NATO intelligence community during the bitter cold-war years of that decade.

By the end of it they knew beyond doubt that they had made the mistake that so many other ambitious men have made, that of specialising too early. Posts that had seemed desirable when they were younger men had, now that they were entering middle age, become dead ends. In the modest hierarchies of the defence establishments to which they belonged they could rise no higher.

It would be easy to see their disenchantment simply as a product of professional frustration and financial disappointment, to paint a picture of disgruntled colonels, barred from further promotion by their own undoubted abilities, underpaid and denied redress, finally becoming sufficiently embittered to take their futures and their fates into their own hands. Such a picture, however, would be out of drawing.

Grievances they certainly had. Their formal responsibilities—and, consequently, their informal powers—had increased substantially over the years without any commensurate advance in rank or pay. Most of their foreign colleagues—not all, but most—held the rank of major general or its equivalent. Attempts by both to have the establishments of their directorates upgraded had invariably failed. These men had not endeared themselves to higher authority; and higher authority, ever wary, was not disposed to make them more influential than they already were. Understandably, they came to prefer civilian dress to their army uniforms. But to conclude that they were driven by their grievances alone and that what they eventually did was merely a bloodyminded expression of accumulated resentments would be to oversimplify their case. Their disenchantment, and the aberration that grew out of it, had deeper origins.

Although Jost and Brand were both professional soldiers, their thinking about war and men had been conditioned not by active service in conventional armies but by what they had learned in resistance movements. The idea that great force can be successfully opposed only by equal or greater force had no meaning for them. To their way of thinking, the way to oppose great force was to find out how to destroy its cohesion and then, when it was fragmented, deal separately with the pieces. They thought, as they had always fought, as guerrillas. They could accept the necessity for the alliance to which their countries were committed. They could accept with resignation the knowledge that their countries meant no more to NATO than Romania or Bulgaria meant to the Warsaw Pact and that they were pygmies involved in a struggle between giants. What they could not do was change their ways of thinking about giants.

They had known the German giant, so omnipotent in his day, and had helped to bring him down. Now, they were able to observe and appraise from peculiar vantage points the American and Russian giants.

The appraisals they made were not flattering. What impressed them most about these giants, they ultimately decided, was not their strength, still less the loud and threatening noises they made, but their inherent clumsiness.

As Brand remarked to Jost one night in Brussels, "They make one think wistfully of dark nights and trip wires."

Their friendship was seven years old when that remark was made and it more or less sums up their attitudes at that stage. They are anti-American as well as anti-Russian. Their talk is subversive, but still only talk. They are dissident, but able to relieve their feelings by indulging in fantasy.

They were meeting officially quite often at that time. Regional intelligence committees had been established, and there were planning conferences in connection with NATO exercises to attend besides.

They looked forward to these occasions, but they were discreet. Both had made other friends among their NATO colleagues and both took care to cultivate them; but with the other friends the professional views they expressed were always carefully orthodox. Their dissidence was a private joke which they had no intention of sharing, even with those who might have proved sympathetic. Their agreement on this point was unspoken, but neither of them ever questioned it. Even at that stage they must have known instinctively that a time would come when they would be glad of their discretion.

From harbouring vague thoughts about the efficacy of trip wires to wondering what they could be made of and where they might be strung is a short step. Jost and Brand began to take that step in 1964.

The meeting place was London and the circumstances were unusual. Tension between the United States and the Soviet Union had eased considerably; the Nuclear Test Ban Treaty had been signed; the hot line between Washington and Moscow had been installed; the reorganisation of NATO was being discussed; the position of France was in doubt; there was change in the air.

Obliged now to examine a new future, Jost and Brand did not much like what they saw. Not that they feared for their posts; they were all too well entrenched in those and could expect to remain so until they reached retirement age; but it was becoming increasingly evident that their importance in the NATO scheme of things, already diminished, was likely soon to become little more than parochial. In a gloomy moment they saw themselves reduced to the role of passive onlookers, of village policemen stationed at minor crossroads on a secret war battlefield where the only effective forces engaged were the big battalions of the CIA and the KGB.

This view of the situation was not altogether fanciful. The CIA and the KGB already operated clandestinely in both their countries. Jost and Brand knew this. They also knew that, beyond keeping themselves informed of their uninvited guests' activities, there was little they could do but register displeasure. They found the CIA's self-righteous assumption that it was not only a welcome guest but also a specially privileged one almost as annoying as the KGB *residenturas'* bland insistence that they did not exist, and just as insulting to the intelligence.

Jost was an overseas member of a London club and it was in the coffee room there that the first of two critical conversations took place.

There had been an unsuccessful attempt early that day to hijack a gold-bullion shipment at London airport, and the evening papers had made it a front-page story. Three of the robbers had already been captured, four others in a second getaway car were being sought, as was the driver of a power-lift truck found abandoned near the scene. Over their brandy, Jost and Brand began idly to discuss the attempt.

"A carefully planned job," commented Brand, "but much too elaborate. I wonder where they got the tear gas. Stolen from an army depot, I suppose."

"Clearly the police had a tip-off."

"Not a very detailed one, though, by the look of things. Five men got away. What is a power-lift truck?"

"I think they are used for delivering heavy objects—machines, refrigerators, things like that. The tail board is power driven and can be raised and lowered vertically like an elevator. Presumably that was going to be used to load the bullion."

"Gold bars worth half a million sterling, it says." Brand thought for a moment. "That would weigh about eleven hundred kilos. Yes, eight men would certainly need help if they expected to load that in a hurry. What idiots!"

"Nothing idiotic about half a million sterling."

"But idiotic to try to take it in gold."

"I don't see why. There is always a market for gold and no need to pay a fence. Any crooked fool can sell gold if he goes to the right places."

"And if he can take the gold with him to these places, yes. Eleven hundred kilos!" Brand snorted. "If I decided to get rich quickly I would choose something lighter to take to the market."

Jost smiled. "Half a million in used banknotes would be lighter, but they would make an awkward parcel."

Brand did not reply immediately. His eyes wandered around the empty room and then returned to Jost. He spoke very quietly now. "For those of us who have access to knowledge," he said, "there are surely other negotiable commodities."

There was another pause. Jost was aware of a sensation in his stomach that he recognized very well, but a sensation with which he had for some years been unfamiliar. He was in the presence of danger again. To reassure himself, to make sure that his friend was joking, he invoked the old formula.

"Don't get me wrong," he said. "I am as eager as the next man to supplement my pension, *but*—" he sighed regretfully—"isn't the special knowledge of the kind we have much too unstable to travel? On such a difficult, dangerous road I would feel safer with liquid nitroglycerine."

Brand did not smile. "There is much special

knowledge that with careful handling can be made safe," he said, "knowledge, moreover, that raises no issues of conscience."

"Oh. Play material, you mean." Jost was relieved but also slightly disappointed. "Play material" was the jargon phrase used to describe the low-grade classified information fed back to the enemy through double agents. It wasn't like Brand to talk nonsense.

Brand shook his head. "No, not play material. Much better than that." He leaned forward. "Hard stuff, but hard stuff that is possibly already shared."

"And therefore probably useless? Oh, I see."

"Useless but not valueless." Brand did smile now. "Just like gold, some might think."

Jost was aware again of the danger sensation, but it was not unpleasant now. "Like gold, perhaps," he said, "but without the market that there is for gold."

"A market could be found, no doubt."

"Can you see us looking for one?"

"No." Brand shrugged. "Perhaps for that sort of commodity the market has to be made." He picked up the evening paper again. "Eight men on the job," he commented, "and there were doubtless as many again involved in the planning and preliminaries. No wonder their security was bad. No wonder the police had a tip-off."

That was all that was said then.

The expected reorganisation took place and official occasions for their private meetings became rarer. Over a year passed before the subject of "access to knowledge" came up again between them. This time it was Jost who raised it.

They were dining at a restaurant in Rome.

Towards the end of dinner Jost said casually: "I heard the other day of a strange commodity sold in an even stranger market."

He saw Brand's eyes flicker over the other tables to see if there was anyone near enough to overhear them, and knew that his friend had not forgotten the earlier conversation. The words *commodity* and *market* had worked as he had hoped they would. Brand's eyes were on his now, still and intent.

"In Mexico," Jost went on, "there is a forger. He is an old man but still very skilful indeed, and he has been practicing his craft successfully for years."

"Successfully? You mean he hasn't been caught?"

"In Mexico he has committed no offence."

"Forgery is not an offence there?"

"Forgery of banknotes, yes. Forgery of bond certificates, of cheques, of other valuable documents of that kind, all those are serious offences, of course. But this old man does not commit them. He forges something different, documents without any face value at all—rare postage stamps with their overprints and cancellations."

Brand raised his eyebrows. "No value, you say?"

"No *face* value. Rare stamps, the very valuable kind, have usually been cancelled by a postmaster and have therefore lost their face value. They are not valid for postage. Their value to international collectors and to those who invest in them lies in their rarity. You know, I dare say, that there are large sums invested in rare stamps."

"Yes." Brand shrugged. "I can see that this would be an amusing and profitable racket for a forger working in Mexico, but I don't quite see . . ."

Jost raised the palm of one hand. "One moment. You don't yet know how profitable it has been for him, nor how amusing." He paused for effect. "The United States Treasury Department has just co-operated in the business of buying him out."

Brand stared. "Are you serious?"

Jost smiled. "It surprised me too. What happened was this. The international stamp dealers had been worried for years by this man's activities. You see, many of these extremely valuable rare stamps are valuable because of the overprints and surcharges superimposed on them. Overprints and surcharges are very much easier to forge than, say, a modern banknote. So, when you get a really skilful man at work, the forgeries are very difficult to detect. That means not only that for the big dealers there has been what amounts to a debasement of their currency, but also that they have been obliged to spend large sums in tracing and exposing the forgeries. They must if they are to protect their own and their clients' investments. Naturally, they, and particularly the Americans, have wanted for some time to do something about the Mexican. But what *could* they do? They had no legal position. When they heard that he was thinking of retiring—he is seventy-six now—they had a new fear. Supposing he sold his plates and equipment to a younger man, or to a group? What then? It didn't bear thinking about. So they decided to pocket their pride and buy him out themselves."

"Where did the Treasury Department come in?"

"Forgery in the United States is a matter for the Treasury Department. The dealers had to have Treasury blessing before they could take what they were buying back into America. An arrangement also had to be made with the U.S. Customs."

"And the blessing was given?"

"Certainly. A secret negotiating committee went down to Mexico to meet with the old man. They not only bought his plates and dies and equipment and records, they also persuaded him to sign an agreement, enforceable in a Mexican court, that he would retire for good. That was for their protection, of course, but it cost them a lot of money. I asked a stamp dealer at home about the case. He told me that it is not unique. A similar thing happened in fifty-three when the British Philatelic Association bought out a French stamp forger named Sperati. Interesting, is it not?"

Jost finished his wine. Absently, Brand reached for the bottle and refilled Jost's glass. With the bottle still poised in the air he looked across the table.

"Nuisance value," he said.

"Precisely."

They said no more until they were back in their hotel; but both had been thinking and they spent the rest of that evening talking of ways in which the lesson of the Mexican forger might be applied by those having their own particular skills and resources. They agreed in the end that there was only one way that could be considered relatively safe. Before they went up to their rooms that night they amused themselves by mapping out a plan of campaign.

Colonel Jost says that he has no idea when the decision to put the plan into action was made.

This was not, I think, an evasion on his part, an attempt to shift the ultimate responsibility onto Brand. In a collusive relationship such as theirs, commitments and decisions are often made obliquely, without discussion, and without anything having been said directly. It is possible, too, that no *formal* decision was ever taken. Theirs was a long-term plan and, in its initial stages certainly, neither of them was called upon to do anything obviously illegal or suspect. A tacit understanding could have carried them to a point of no return, or at any rate to a point at which return would have seemed to them anticlimactic and ridiculous.

So, the moment when the private joke turned into a conspiracy passed unnoticed by those who conspired. They were not given to self-examination. All they knew, or cared, was that in Rome that year they had found a new game to play and that it would be more stimulating, perhaps more profitable, than the old.

As the steamer left the quay at Vevey, Brand came out of the saloon and went to the upper deck.

Jost was sitting near the rail. After a moment or two Brand strolled over and sat down beside him.

For a full minute they stared out at the lake in silence. A casual observer would have put them down as respectable business or professional men in their late fifties; a perceptive one might have guessed from their clothes that they were foreign to Switzerland, but not from the same country; nobody would have thought it odd that they should start talking to each other rather than look at the scenery. On that cold, windy day the beauties of Lac Léman were not much in evidence.

"What is your cover in Evian?" It was Jost who spoke first.

"The best." Brand stared out at the slate-grey lake. "There is a doctor in Evian who specialises in diseases of the kidneys. I had reason to consult him."

"My friend, I'm sorry. I hope he has given you good news."

"Not good. Not quite as bad as I had expected, but not good. I am afraid that our business has now become a matter of urgency."

Jost turned to look at him.

"In three months I must retire," Brand said.

"For reasons of health?"

"Yes."

"This is a sad blow." Jost drew his coat collar closer around his neck. "Personally, I detest sympathy. I would think that it is the same with you."

"Yes. I did not propose this meeting merely to talk of trouble. I have more interesting news. Fortune appears at last to be smiling on us."

"Fortune?"

Brand slid a hand into his overcoat breast pocket. "I think we can now take the steps necessary to activate our joint investment."

His hand reappeared with a slip of paper. He passed it to Jost.

Jost saw that it was an obituary clipped from the

European edition of an American news magazine. It read:

> DIED. Brigadier General Luther B. Novak, 62, U.S. Army (Ret.), lecturer, publisher of the international weekly newsletter *Intercom* and patron saint of the far-out, millionaire-backed Interform Foundation; of a heart attack; in Geneva. His premature retirement from the Army in 1955 followed GI complaints to Congressmen of his attempts to indoctrinate U.S. troops in Germany with his own political views, the extremity of which, according to one witness at the inquiry, "made the John Birch Society look like parlor pinks." His subsequent career as publisher, polemicist and self-styled "controller of a world-wide private spy network" was marked by further brushes with authority, notably the State Department and the CIA. A harassed deputy director of that agency was once driven to describing the *Intercom* newsletter and its gadfly proprietor as "an international migraine headache airmailed weekly by a latter-day Titus Oates."

Jost passed the cutting back. He hid his disappointment behind a polite nod.

"I had heard that Novak was dead," he said; "but the newsletter is controlled by this foundation, surely."

"That is what I thought," Brand replied; "but it is so exactly the sort of thing we had in mind, that, with my time running out, I thought it worthwhile to make further inquiries. What I found was interesting. The foundation is run as sort of a hobby by three wealthy, rather stupid men who think they are fighting world communism. They subsidise the making of documentary films, recorded radio and television programmes for free distribution, and the writing of unreadable but expensive-looking books and pamphlets. They pay the wages of a staff working on anti-communist research, whatever that may be, and they retain a firm of public-relations counsellors. They paid Novak a salary and expenses for his work as organiser of the foundation. But they do not run the *Intercom* newsletter. That was Novak's personal property. He started it, after he resigned from the American Army, with money left to him by his wife. He used up most of that inheritance. *Intercom* lost money for several years, and, in spite of its circulation and notoriety since, it has never done better than break even. He had his army pension, of course, but, until he met these rich idiots who backed the foundation, most of his income came from lecturing."

"Then who owns *Intercom* now?"

Brand gave his friend a sidelong look. "I hope that we do."

Jost drew a deep breath. "You must forgive me," he said. "For a moment there I doubted."

"I know." Brand smiled. "I have not often surprised you. I was tempted to try. I say I *hope* it is ours. It should be by next week if all goes well. The position is this. Intercom Publishing Enterprises A.G. is a Swiss corporation registered in Zug and directed, in order to conform with the Swiss code, by a Swiss national. He is a lawyer in Bâle. The shares, ninety-seven per cent of which were owned by Novak, are now part of his estate. This goes to a married daughter living in Baltimore in the United States. Through our cut-out I have made an offer for the shares of ten thousand dollars. Since the only assets are the lease of an office suite in Geneva, one Addressograph and two duplicating machines, two typewriters and some highly questionable good will, ten thousand is about twice what the shares are worth. I heard two days ago that the daughter in Baltimore is likely to accept the offer. Pending confirmation of her acceptance, the *Intercom* lawyer has undertaken to see that the

Geneva staff salaries are paid and that publication continues."

"Has Novak's death not affected it at all? Who is writing the thing now?"

"The same man who has been writing it for the past four years. His name is Theodore Carter. Novak was never much more than a figurehead. He always had to have someone to do the actual work."

"But what about the material? Where does that come from? Crude invention may account for some of it, but there is much circumstantial stuff. Even *Intercom* must have sources. What is this 'private spy network' he boasted about?"

Brand grinned. "Paper mills," he said.

Jost grimaced sourly. "Paper mills" was the term they and their colleagues used to describe the innumerable political warfare and propaganda groups engaged in feeding misinformation to the international news-gathering agencies. Some paper mills had government subsidies, others were financed by émigré organisations and separatist movements; a few of the smaller, more furtive paper mills—those, for instance, which specialised in the manufacture of false intelligence documents—were businesses run for profit. Since the output of the paper mills had always to be evaluated—the kind of misinformation being propagated by an opponent could sometimes give an indication of his true intentions—the work load they created was a perennial source of inconvenience to intelligence agencies.

"This Theodore Carter," said Jost; "where did he come from? Is he one of the paper-mill hacks?"

"Not exactly. His predecessor at *Intercom* was certainly one of those. Felix Kortan, you may remember him. An American-educated Hungarian who operated after the war in Vienna. Called himself a Russian expert. Even Novak saw through his faking eventually. Carter is a little better than that, I think. I have seen a fairly thorough report on him."

"I would like to see that report, if possible."

"I can tell you the essentials now." Brand half closed his eyes. "Theodore Carter. No middle name. Aged fifty-five, a Canadian citizen born in Montreal. Educated there and in France. Married a French woman from whom he is now divorced. A daughter, Valerie, aged twenty-three, lives with him and is an assistant librarian employed at the University of Geneva. Carter has spent most of his adult life as a working journalist, mainly in French-speaking countries. He is a French-English bilingual and proficient in German and Italian. His best period—by 'best' I mean the period when he behaved more or less as an educated man of his age should, and when he drank least—was the six years prior to the break-up of his marriage. He worked in the Paris office of a British news agency for four of them, and then in the news department there of an American radio and television network."

"Is he an alcoholic?"

"He has what our American friends call a drinking problem. Not an alcoholic, but certainly a heavy drinker. The report describes him as being flawed, a man of undoubted ability who takes pleasure in misusing it."

"And so, while wallowing in self-pity, drinks. I see. Is he himself an extreme anti-communist?"

"The judgment is that he is capable of being extremely anti-anything, as long as the pay is good. It proved impossible to discover whether or not he had private political convictions different from those of his employer. Since Novak appears to have trusted him completely, he is undoubtedly capable of putting on a convincing act when it suits him to do so."

"Has anyone ever attempted to recruit this man?"

"I suppose the CIA looked him over when he worked for the American radio people in Paris. They would do so normally. Probably the drinking put them off. There was nothing in the report."

Brand paused. "Is your part of the operation ready?"

"It can soon be made ready, but I will have to move quickly." Jost stared ahead. They were approaching the pier at Ouchy-Lausanne now, and in a few minutes he would have to leave. "I think I may stay in this area for a further twenty-four hours," he said.

"And visit Geneva?"

"I would like to see things for myself." Jost hesitated. "This is going to be a little dangerous for Carter," he said.

Brand pursed his lips. "Well, yes. A *little* dangerous perhaps. But that was always an implicit side effect."

"Implicit, yes, but we have never really discussed the problem."

"What is there to discuss?" Having said all that he had come there to say, Brand was tiring now. "Once your *démarche* begins there will be dangerous moments for Carter. We must accept that. We cannot protect him."

"No, of course not. It would be ill-advised to try. We might perhaps, though, warn him."

"Impossible. A man like that? He would just leave. The whole operation would be aborted." Brand drew breath. "No, it is all a calculated risk. He must take his chance. It may be unpleasant for him, but it will not be so for long. They will soon realise that he knows nothing, that he is an innocent."

Jost looked at the grey face and decided to say no more. In any case there was no time left; the steamer was edging in towards the pier. He stood up.

"My friend," he said, "all my congratulations on your work for us. I hope that my own part will be as effective."

"Of course it will. You will send me a progress report?"

"In the usual way. Take care of yourself. I hope your family are all well."

"Yes, yes, all well."

They touched hands briefly, surreptitiously, and then Jost walked aft, down to the gangway where he would disembark.

THREE

FROM THEODORE CARTER
(transcribed dictation tape)

I think I'll call you Mr. L. L for Latimer, Lewison, lubricious and *louche*.

Well, Mr. L, you'd better watch yourself; your sheep's clothing is slipping. When I agreed to co-operate with you I had to listen to a lot of sanctimonious jazz about probity, good faith and strict adherence to proven fact. I thought at the time that it smelt a bit of overcompensation, but I didn't think the gilt would wear off the gingerbread quite so soon. I gave it a month. But no: two weeks.

Mr. L, I don't very much mind your appropriating a privately dictated tape from my former secretary, Nicole Deladoey, and transcribing it without my permission; after all, you're paying the cow's wages now, and so presumably have purchased her loyalty along with her services. *That was a bitchy trick, Nicole.* I don't even mind your wide-eyed and patently dishonest contention that, in reproducing that tape unedited, you were merely honouring retroactively a term of our agreement that *I* had insisted upon; that's the kind of probity and good faith we men of the world can all understand. What I do object to, and object strongly, is your slipping in flagrant distortions of fact.

We'd better get this straight. I don't know what

38

half-baked sources you've been tapping for this gossip and hearsay. You can't tell me that you got it all out of "Colonel Jost," though I suppose that some of it *must* be hard or not even *you* would dare.

By the way, I will admit that the scene where those two old buzzards are mumbling over the evening paper and thinking about play material and pension plans still reads as if it could have happened. Schadenfreude *is the word you wanted for their kind of bloodymindedness, but maybe it eluded you. Cut down on the adjectives and adverbs, Mr. L; purple is out this season.*

Where was I?

Oh yes. Facts. Now look. As I say, I don't know anything about these sources of yours or how much you've paid them, but if that little character-assassination vignette of me which you've now added is a fair sample of what you've been getting, I'll tell you something. You're stuck with a bag of lemons. I was taught always to check and double-check information received before starting to think of it as fact. I think you should have checked with me first, Mr. L. Maybe I don't know everything about myself, but I do know a few things. Or was it too tasty as it was to risk spoiling with a dash of truth?

Cooperation is a two-way street, Mr. L. I do not like that reference to my drinking. It is not only untrue but damaging to my reputation. I want it deleted from the text. Get it right, Mr. L, get it right. I do not drink heavily. I drink what I *need* to drink. The need *varies* from time to time. It's that simple.

The night the General turned in his chips is a case in point. As what happened that night had a distinct effect on the attitudes of the police and security people towards me later, you'd better know about it.

The General got into Geneva at about five-thirty

that afternoon on a delayed Swissair flight from New York. As usual, I met him at the airport and drove him to his hotel.

I always got on well with the General. You say, or make one of those old bastards say, that I put on an act with him. Well, of course I did. With him you couldn't do anything else but put on an act. Talking to him was like talking to a kid who's playing a game of cowboys and Indians; unless you want to spoil the fun you have to go along with him. The name of the General's game wasn't cowboys and Indians but something a little more complicated; let's say, "good spies, bad spies and international plots." The effect, though, was the same. He wasn't interested in reality. No, that's wrong. He believed that the game he played *was* reality and that anyone who doubted this was either a good guy living in a dream world or a bad guy trying to lull the good guys into a sense of false security. He was a crackpot, of course, a nut, but in his way a very impressive one. I only heard him lecture once; it was at the American Club here. He was a terrible ham; he waved dossiers and quoted phony facts and figures by the yard; everything he said was complete balls; but, my God, he was effective. You see, he really *believed* what he was saying.

He was great at starting hares. For him, anything that happened, simply anything, could be part of a plot or conspiracy. The smallest thing would set him off. Then away he'd go, piling suspicion on suspicion, twisting the facts if there were any, imagining them if there weren't, until he had arrived at what he decided was the truth of the matter. Then I'd write it up and we'd print it.

No wonder they got mad at us in Washington. Every Senator and every Congressman—every Canadian and British M.P., too, for that matter—got a copy of *Intercom,* whether they paid their subscriptions or not. You'd be surprised how many of those hares we started ran and kept on running.

Well, maybe *you* wouldn't be surprised. You know a bit about politicians. They got so steamed up in Washington about one story we ran—some crap we'd cooked up about the range of a new Red Chinese nuclear missile delivery system—that the President himself had to issue a denial. That didn't faze the General, of course. He loved denials. All he did was cable me to run the story again along with additional supporting evidence. He didn't say where this additional supporting evidence was to come from, of course; that wasn't his way. And, of course, I didn't waste time asking questions. As the whole of the original supporting evidence had been dreamed up, obviously any additional supporting evidence would have to be dreamed up, too. Naturally, I'd never have used a phrase like "dreamed up" to him. That would have been like saying that good guys rode black horses. He believed what he wanted to believe, and he always knew that whatever he imagined counted as evidence.

He was still imagining when he died. That last time I drove him from the airport he started talking about an item he'd read in a magazine on the plane. The item said that there was an outfit called the World Meteorological Organisation and that they had an advisory committee examining the consequences of large-scale interference with the atmosphere.

"How do you like that, Ted?" he said darkly.

I played it down; I knew the signs and I didn't want to be up all night. "Something to do with cloud-seeding, isn't it, General?" I said. "A plane drops dry ice or some chemical into a cloud and that makes it rain. Nice for the farmer whose land's underneath, not so good for the farmer who'd have had that cloud later."

But he wasn't put off. "No, Ted. There's more to it than that. *Large-scale* interference with our atmosphere, that's what it said. I want the inside stuff on this World Meteorological Organisation and the way it operates, and I want it fast. I think we ought to dig deep here."

Once he'd started talking about digging deep there was no holding him. Usually, when we got to the hotel, we'd have a few drinks in his suite before dinner, but that evening he was high on the WMO and I had to go chasing off to see what we had on it in the office.

I found a piece about rainmaking and the WMO in a scientific yearbook. There wasn't much to it. A paper had been prepared discussing the possibilities for international cooperation in research in the field of cloud and precipitation physics. As a result of this paper, the WMO Commission for Aerology (whatever that is) had created a working group of scientists to take the thing a stage further. An international conference under the auspices of the International Union of Geodesy and Geophysics was to be held shortly.

Not much, as I say, but enough for the General. Repetition of the word "international" always stirred him up. Once his eagle eye had noted that the author of the discussion paper was Professor L. Krastanov of Bulgaria and that the working group included not only Krastanov but also V. T. Nilandrov of the Soviet Union, he was off and running. The fact that the group also included professors from Arizona, India and Japan was brushed aside with the instruction that we should run checks on their personal histories and political backgrounds. By nine o'clock that night the General was all set to expose yet another communist plot to destroy the free world, this time by changing its climate and lousing up its weather, so that all those rich farmlands—"heartlands," he called them—would be turned into dust bowls and deserts.

Go easy on the water this time, Val.

It was about then that he complained of indigestion. Shortly afterwards he went to the bathroom and threw up. He came out looking very bad and said that something was squeezing his chest. He was obviously in pain and said that he had been poisoned. I made him lie down in the bedroom, then rang down to the concierge and told him to call the hotel doctor. I was thinking that he might have a duodenal ulcer that was acting up.

The General was well known at that hotel and the doctor came promptly. He diagnosed a heart attack and called for an ambulance. By nine-thirty that evening the General was in a *polyclinique* bed wearing an oxygen mask. According to the hospital doctor I spoke to, his condition was critical.

"How critical?" I asked.

Doctors hate questions like that. "It is too early to say yet," he said, "but serious damage has been done. It would be wise perhaps to notify his relatives."

That put me in a quandary. I told him, "The only relative I know of, Doctor, is a daughter in America. I'll cable her, naturally, but I can't just tell her he's had a heart attack and leave it at that. Maybe I can telephone her. But what do I say? Should she get on the first plane out or what?"

He hesitated before he answered. "We will know more later, in an hour or two perhaps when his condition is stabilised. I suggest you wait or, better, come back later."

I told him I would come back later.

I had travelled in the ambulance to the hospital, so my car was still parked back at the hotel. If I'd had it with me I might have gone home for a while. As it was, I walked back to the hotel, got the car, drove back to the hospital, parked and went into a bar to wait.

I did have quite a few brandies there, I don't mind admitting it. I had them because I needed them.

In my trade you learn to listen not just to what people say, but also to how they are saying it—the music as well as the words, so to speak. Doctors are not always as good at covering up as they think. I'd already guessed that the General's chances of lasting the night were not much better than evens. Which meant, in turn, that my chances of being out of a job in the near future were not much better than evens.

"Colonel Brand," as you call him, was quite right when he said that *Intercom* didn't show a profit. Not many of these newsletter-type "personalized intelligence services" do—not directly, that is. Most of them are in business for reasons other than the ostensible one of giving inside information. All kinds of reasons: to make enemies and influence people, to smear political opponents—try suing a newsletter—to rig stock prices, to plant misinformation from a paper mill—all kinds: rational, irrational, sinister and plain stupid. But, when the reason goes, the newsletter usually goes with it.

In the case of *Intercom* the reason was that the General wanted to bug the people who had made him resign from the army and, at the same time, jack up his lecture-tour fees by publicising himself as the great anti-communist Free World crusader. My guess was, then, that if the General were to die, *Intercom* would not long survive him. I didn't see the foundation taking over. The General had always kept them well out of the Geneva picture. They didn't even know that I ghosted the whole thing for him; they had started off believing that he wrote it all himself and he had let them go on believing that he did. Even if I could have set them straight on that score, I doubted if they would have been interested in keeping *me* on. One of those old oil-money weirdos had once turned up in Geneva on a European tour; in an expansive moment I had told him that the name Interform Foundation sounded to me like an ad for women's girdles. It hadn't gone down well and word had been passed on to the other weirdos. Back at the foundation I was bad news.

So I sat in that bar near the hospital, contemplating my uncertain future and drinking brandy.

I returned to the hospital just before midnight. In case I had to wait about there, I took along a couple of nip-size bottles with me.

It was two o'clock in the morning when a nurse came to me in the waiting room and asked me to go with her to the administration office. There, the doctor I had seen earlier told me that the General had died.

There was another, younger white-smock in the office, too, and a man in civilian clothes whom I took to be a hospital official. All three of them were looking very formal and starchy. It didn't occur to me to wonder why. After all, when a death in a hospital emergency ward is announced, you don't expect a lot of merry smiles and back-slapping. I was feeling lousy, of course, but I tried to be businesslike.

"I will cable the news to his daughter immediately," I said. "She will have to be consulted about the funeral arrangements, too. I will also notify his lawyer. As the General was a United States citizen, an American consul should probably be told, too. The nearest one's in Bern, I think. I don't know if you do that or whether you want me to. I can, of course. In the meantime . . ."

I ran out of gas for a moment there. What I had really been getting around to asking him was whether he could just hold everything until someone who knew what you did in Geneva with the bodies of retired American brigadier generals could take over; but he didn't give me a chance to finish.

"In the meantime, Monsieur," he said stiffly, "there has been a question raised as to the cause of death."

"A question? I thought you said he had a heart attack."

"An acute myocardial infarction. Yes, that was our diagnosis."

"Well, then, who's questioned it?"

"The deceased questioned it himself. Twice." He looked at the other white-smock for confirmation and got a nod. "He was under sedation, of course, but during the periods of consciousness perfectly lucid. He twice stated that someone had poisoned him."

That was the moment when I should have mentioned the indigestion he'd complained of after dinner, suggested diffidently that what the General had obviously been talking about was *food* poisoning, and thereafter kept my mouth shut.

I did none of these things; and I didn't do them (a) because I was upset, (b) because I disliked the doctor's manner, (c) because I was a mite loaded and (d) because I was curious. I wanted to know who it was that the General *in extremis* had fingered as the bad guy. My money was on the World Meteorological Organisation.

So I thought I'd ask. "Did he accuse anyone in particular?"

He gave me a beady look. "You do not seem surprised that he should make such statements."

"Why should I be surprised?" I said. "He'd already made that statement about being poisoned twice before we got here, once after he'd been taken ill and then later in the ambulance."

That did it. He stiffened up as if I had goosed him. "Why did you not report this when the patient was received here?"

"Because he obviously didn't know what he was talking about. The hotel doctor had diagnosed a heart attack. Why should I question it? What is all this nonsense?"

He didn't like that. "This nonsense, as you call it, is a serious matter, Monsieur. You must realise that it will now be necessary for us to perform an autopsy."

"Oh, for God's sake." I had had no great sentimental regard for the General, but the idea of his being disembowelled merely in order to clear up an idiotic misunderstanding was too much. I said so in no uncertain terms. I dare say I wasn't very polite.

The doctor bridled. "In cases where doubts have been raised as to the cause of a sudden death," he said loudly, "we have no choice. An autopsy becomes mandatory and we are required to inform the police."

"Even when the doubts are irrational?"

"Who can say at this moment whether they are irrational or not?" The man in the civilian suit had chipped in now. He was fortyish, thin, with a narrow head and fish-blue eyes.

"This," said the doctor grimly, "is Monsieur Vauban of the judiciary police."

If I had had the sense then to keep quiet and let things take their course, I might, even at that late stage, have emerged as a fairly okay character— tetchy and lacking in tact, perhaps, but basically sane and accountable. But I was too exasperated to keep quiet. I had an irresistible urge to explain to those fatheads what had made the General tick.

"Look," I said, "I know it's difficult for people like you to understand anything outside your own immediate experience, but I'll try and spell it out for you. *Nil nisi bonum* and all that, but the General was, to put it mildly, a bit eccentric. He subscribed to the conspiratorial theory of history, if you know what that is—*all* history, including his own. If you want to be medical about it you might say that his attitude was consistently paranoid. I'll ask you a question. When there's a flu epidemic, do you start suspecting the Russians of waging biological warfare? No? Well, he did. Has it ever occurred to you that the current attempts to develop electric and steam-driven automobiles are all part of an international plot to destroy the capitalist system? No? Well, the General could make out a very good case for it. He had not one bee in his bonnet, but hundreds. If he were here now, do you know what he'd be saying? I'll tell you. He'd say that there had been a plot to murder him and that it had triumphantly succeeded."

There was a dead silence. The policeman looked at me as if I'd been pleading guilty to indecent exposure. Obviously, he wasn't receiving the message I was trying to send, or else misunderstanding it. I tried again, using an analogy that I thought might get through to him.

"Don't you see what I mean? Common sense suggests that the murder was an inside job and that the killers were high blood pressure, cholesterol, hypertension and so on. A mundane theory, I'm afraid. The General wouldn't have given it the time of day. How can it have been an inside job when there are all those cunning devils creeping about *outside,* plotting, planning, with phials of little-known poisons in their pockets along with their CP membership cards? And who did these fiends want to destroy most? Who else but their arch-enemy, that great Free World crusader for truth, your friend and mine, Luther B. Novak? That's how his mind worked. You see?"

From the blank stares it was clear that they did not see. It took me a few moments to realise that, without thinking, I had at some point switched from French to English. I back-tracked and started to give them the last bit again in French, but the policeman stopped me.

"Please, Monsieur. You are wasting time—your own, mine, and certainly the hospital's. I believe that you were with the deceased continually from the time he arrived in Geneva until he was taken ill."

"I was."

"Then I would have thought that, in view of the

allegations of poisoning that have been made, you would certainly not oppose an autopsy and might even welcome it."

I could have hit him. "Are you saying now that *I* am a suspect?"

"Until the results of the autopsy are known, the question of suspicion does not arise." He smiled unpleasantly. "However, I note that your late employer was not alone in his eccentricity."

That got a short laugh from the doctor. I turned to go. By that time I no longer cared what they did with the General. I just wanted to get out of that place.

"One moment, Monsieur." It was the policeman again. "Your papers, please."

I gave him my residence permit. He thumbed the pages slowly. He didn't take notes, but he was obviously memorising. He handed it back reluctantly as if disappointed that there didn't appear to be anything wrong with it. His nod of dismissal was reluctant too. He wouldn't forget about me. In Monsieur Vauban's book I was trouble.

It was Dr. Bruchner, the General's lawyer in Bâle, who told me the result of the autopsy.

The General had died of "congestive heart failure following acute myocardial infarction due to coronary occlusion." A death certificate was issued by the hospital, and a few hours later the body was flown to America for burial. A man from the American consulate was there when Dr. Bruchner and I saw the coffin off at the freight department of the airport.

Before he returned to Bâle, Dr. Bruchner told me that he was in touch with the General's executors in America and that until he heard further from them I was to carry on. He knew, of course, that I had always written the *Intercom* newsletter practically singlehanded; but he also knew, as I did, that without the General's name on the thing, it wouldn't amount to much. We agreed on a formula to cover the new situation. In place of the General's signature there would be the words: *From* INTERCOM *World Intelligence Network,* Novak Editorial Unit, Geneva. In the obituary I was to do on the General I would try to sell the idea that, although *he* might be dead, the network he had founded was still very much alive, and that *Intercom* would continue to bear aloft the torch of freedom. Dr. Bruchner didn't actually advise me in so many words to start looking for another job, but his kindly smile as he told me to use my own judgment and do the best I could had much the same effect.

Two weeks went by. Then I had a letter from Dr. Bruchner saying that the American executors had decided to sell out. They had also stated that, as the General had thought so highly of me, an offer from me personally for the shares would receive specially sympathetic consideration.

Dr. Bruchner knew too much about *Intercom's* financial position, and mine, to comment on that suggestion. He did, though, ask whether I had any ideas about possible buyers. From the way he phrased that part of the letter I gathered that he hadn't any ideas at all. He also said that there wasn't much time. I didn't have to be told that. *Intercom* had always lived a hand-to-mouth existence on subscriptions, and, since the General's death, all we'd had in were a few renewals from people who had probably forgotten to tell their secretaries or business managers to cancel. I gave it two months before Dr. Bruchner decided to write to the executors recommending that Intercom Publishing Enterprises A.G. be placed in liquidation.

I talked it over with Val. That's Valerie, my daughter.

She's as beautiful as her mother was when I first met her; but there's none of that bitchiness in Val. She works, as your assiduous legmen discov-

ered, Mr. L. as a librarian at the university. I won't
say more about her now. If you have any sense
you'll be letting her speak for herself. She won't
let me down. One word of warning, though. Val
has some funny ideas. Don't let that psychiatrist
boyfriend of hers get into the act. He's not a bad
young man—just a nonswimmer working as a life-
guard.

No, better scrub that. He did at least try to help.

As I say, I talked things over with Val.
To be truthful. I must say that I wasn't looking
for much more from her than daughterly sympathy
and concern. All that about my wallowing in self-
pity is for the birds, Mr. L. I also felt that I had
to let her know what the score was. If I had to get
another job, I thought, it would almost certainly
mean that I would have to leave Geneva. That
would have affected her future. I felt that she ought
to have time to think and make plans.
Somewhat to my surprise, she came up with a
plan for me.
Geneva, of course, is the headquarters of all sorts
of international organisations and there are always
conferences going on. I don't mean just the political
junkets, but conferences concerned with international cooperation in technical fields. Since Val had
been working for the university she had become
aware of the shortage that existed of technical trans-
lators able to service such conferences. I don't
mean interpreters; there are plenty of those, though
not many good verbatim technical interpreters; I
mean people who can produce accurate and reliable
translations of technical documents fast enough to
keep a conference supplied with multilingual copies
of minutes, papers read and so on while it is still in
session. Her idea was that, if Intercom Publishing
Enterprises A.G. went into liquidation, I should
buy up the pieces, selling the *Intercom* mailing list

and the Addressograph machine to help finance the deal, but keeping the office lease and furniture, the typewriters and the mimeograph machines in order to set up a technical translation bureau.

It wasn't a bad idea, I thought. I didn't think it would work, but it was good to have something to hope for and speculate about. I only had two drinks that evening.

Ten days later I had a telephone call from Dr. Bruchner.

"I have received an offer for the General's shareholding," he said. He sounded as if he could still hardly believe it.

"A good offer, I hope." I tried not to echo his incredulity.

"Good enough, I think, to submit to the executors."

"May I ask who has made the offer?"

"Ah. That is why I am calling you. You may be able to help me. The prospective purchaser is Herr Arnold Bloch of Munich. His business paper states that he is an industrial public-relations consultant. In his initial letter inquiring about the availability of the shares he stated that he is acting in concert with French and West German associates with interests in arms and explosives. I gathered that his expectation is that he will be able to use *Intercom* to promote his associates' commercial interests."

"That sounds good. It makes sense. If they are prepared to subsidise it out of their advertising appropriations, they're obviously not counting on us to show a profit. They're buying in with their eyes open and a policy in mind."

"That was my thought also."

"How can I help, Dr. Bruchner?"

"In cabling this offer to the executors, I would like to give some assurances that Herr Bloch is a responsible person."

"Can he back his offer with cash?"

"Monsieur Carter, please!" The question had hurt

him; I should have known better than to ask it. "Naturally that was the first thing I established. I have a cashier's draft on his Munich bank already in my possession. He is certainly financially responsible. The assurance I wish to give is that he is politically responsible, the kind of person who would not have been objectionable to the General."

"I see."

"Unfortunately, I know very little about Herr Bloch. He seems to be a thoughtful and considerate person. For instance, he has specifically requested me to assure you that he hopes to retain your services, and those of your staff, should his offer for the shares be accepted."

"Good for him. Then isn't that your answer? If he likes *Intercom* as it is, he can't be politically objectionable in the way you mean, can he? I take it that all he wants to do is slip in a few commercial plugs from time to time."

"I understand that. But . . ."

"What sort of a man is he personally?"

"That is the difficulty. I have corresponded with him and we have spoken on the telephone, but I have not actually had occasion to meet him. He is an educated man clearly. His German is fluent, though I think that he is not himself German-born."

"Austrian perhaps?"

"Perhaps. I don't know. I made preliminary inquiries about him through my Munich correspondent, but learned very little. He has an office at the address given on his business paper, and there is a plate on the door saying that he has offices also in Paris and Rome. That is also stated on the paper, but no addresses are given. Apparently he travels a great deal on his clients' behalf. He employs no permanent staff in Munich. The office rent is paid by the bank."

"He sounds like what the Americans call an operator, or a front man. That's not necessarily against him, of course."

"No." Dr. Bruchner did his best not to sound dubious. "Before I send this cable," he went on, "will you try to find out more? You have files and dossiers, I know, and are experienced in these matters. I would like to be able to say in my cable that investigation has uncovered nothing to his discredit."

"I understand, Dr. Bruchner. I'll do what I can and call you back later."

What I could in fact do was very little. The files and dossiers to which he referred were mostly figments of the General's imagination. We had some filing cabinets, true, and they were full of paper—files of old newspaper cuttings, roughly indexed—but it was all very ordinary stuff. We did have a fair reference library, and I kept special scrapbooks containing ideas and material for *Intercom* stories culled from the European newspapers and magazines to which we subscribed; but we had no proper morgue in the newspaper sense of the term. That sort of thing needs space and a trained staff; and it costs money.

The last thing I wanted at that stage, of course, was to uncover anything to Herr Bloch's discredit; and I assumed that Dr. Bruchner was of the same mind. His fee as director of Intercom Publishing Enterprises A.G. wasn't all that big, but obviously he would prefer not to lose it.

I did make inquiries about Arnold Bloch, however.

There was nothing about him in any of the standard reference books, so I looked him up in the list of *Intercom* subscribers. I did that because I thought that there might possibly be an address for him there different from the Munich address Dr. Bruchner had given me.

Big surprise. Arnold Bloch didn't subscribe to *Intercom* and never had done.

Well, you could scarcely count that as being to his discredit. Some people might even have said that it was an indication of good sense on his part. But,

even allowing for the fact that this prospective purchaser was acting for unidentified French and German associates, it was, I thought, odd. After all,
he was the publicity consultant who hoped to use
Intercom to promote his associates' commercial interests; *he* was the thoughtful and considerate man
of affairs who wanted *Intercom* to stay in business
as usual. How come he had never subscribed to it?
The oddity made me curious enough to make a
further inquiry. I put in a call to Paris to the woman
who ran the morgue at the news-agency bureau I'd
worked in there. We'd always got on well and she
never minded doing me a favour. This favour didn't
take long to do. There were several Blochs listed in
her file index, but none of them was an Arnold
Bloch.

Again, nothing to his discredit.

There was one more source I could have tried. In
most big cities there are agencies which make their
livings by taking photographs of business executives
for free and then holding the negatives in the expectation that, sooner or later, some of those men will
become news. Then the agency sells ten-by-eight
glossies to the newspapers and magazines. As an
industrial public-relations consultant, Arnold Bloch
would, I thought have rated that sort of attention.
Somewhere, no doubt, there was a picture of Herr
Bloch ready to be pulled out and used if he ever
distinguished himself by getting killed in an air
crash, marrying a film star or becoming involved in
a multimillion-dollar take-over bid. I didn't think,
though, that the picture, even if I could find it
quickly, would tell me anything useful. Even the
good guys sometimes have their eyes set far too
closely together.

So, in the end, I just called Dr. Bruchner back
and told him that, as far as I could see, Herr
Arnold Bloch was as clean as a whistle. He said
that he would send off the cable to the executors
that night.

The date was October 26.

Now, Mr. L, I have news for you.

You've been so bloody secretive about your sources that it's difficult to know how much credence can be given to the details of your reconstruction. But I will say this. If the last section of that lake-steamer conversation between the old buzzards is basically factual, you're in for something of a shock. Better fasten your seat belt. There's something you don't know.

On November 1, one week after that cable to the executors went off, something peculiar happened in the office. Nicole was there and can confirm this. I had a strange visitor.

It was in the afternoon. When I got back from lunch I found this man waiting there. Nothing particularly unusual about that, of course. We didn't have many callers at the office, but we had some: office-supplies salesmen, bill collectors, odd characters looking for jobs and two-bit con men trying to flog secret documents cooked up in some Berlin kitchen. The unusual thing about this particular caller was that he was there to take out a subscription to *Intercom*.

Now that really *was* unusual. Certainly, it had never happened before while I was there. *Intercom* went out by mail and that's how the subscriptions came in. We had a mimeographed subscription form giving the different rates to Europe and the Americas in the various currencies; and one of these forms was always tacked onto the newsletter, or enclosed with a renewal notice. From time to time we'd had promotional mailings using the same form; but, even the Geneva subscribers, and there were one or two, had never come to the office in person.

Naturally, my first thought when he told me what he wanted was that this must be Arnold Bloch, or someone connected with him, there to give our little outfit a discreet onceover. True, if this *were* Bloch, he'd left things a bit late. Dr. Bruchner already had his cheque, and if the written offer he'd made was accepted the deal was done. Even if he didn't like what he saw it was too late for him to renege now. Still, whoever or whatever he was, the kid-glove treatment was clearly in order. Very politely I asked him into my office and told Nicole to bring in a subscription form.

What with the reference library, the scrapbooks and the stacks of magazines and newspapers in my office, there was scarcely room to move, but I did have a visitor's chair. The General had insisted on that. It was piled high with junk, as usual. While I was clearing it the visitor stood in the doorway taking off his overcoat and folding it up neatly as if he were going to pack it.

He was of average height and thick-set with a very straight back. I put him in the middle fifties. A rather heavy face; I don't mean flabby—there was nothing flabby about him; he looked as hard as nails—but big-boned, with prominent jaw muscles. "Craggy" is probably the word. The eyes behind the acetate-rimmed bifocals were blue, the short, wiry hair was grey, the complexion a faded summer tan; and on his wide, thin-lipped mouth there rested a regretful little smile. The smile, I soon found, was permanent and the regret it seemed to express illusory.

As he sat down in the chair I had cleared, Nicole brought in the subscription form. I handed him a ballpoint pen. He studied the form for a moment, then began to fill it in, in block letters as requested.

I could read the name he gave upside down. It was Werner Siepen. The address was a *Postfach* number in Hamburg. The separate spaces provided for business address and occupation he left blank. His signature was illegible.

Not Arnold Bloch, then, but he could conceivably be one of the West German clients for whom Bloch was acting. There was nothing unusual about his omitting to give his occupation. Few of our sub-scribers—the commonest exceptions were politi-cians, clergymen and, for some mysterious reason, dentists—chose or bothered to fill that line in. But I was, for obvious reasons, specially curious about this one. I tried to get him to open up a bit.

"The yearly subscription rate for Germany is eighty marks," I said. "No doubt you would prefer to pay by cheque. Most of our subscribers do."

He shrugged. "Cash would be simpler, I think—" he reached for his wallet— "and Swiss francs sim-pler still." His French was quite good.

"As you please. I will have the German rate con-verted and a receipt made out." I pressed the buzzer for Nicole and offered him a cigarette.

He refused the cigarette with a graceful twitch of the hundred-franc note he had produced and then placed the note on top of the subscription form. While I was giving Nicole the necessary instruc-tions he took a Dutch panatella from his pocket and lit that. He seemed to be in no hurry. That was fine with me.

"It is not often," I said, "that we have the op-portunity of meeting our subscribers face to face. Many write to us, of course, but . . ."

"Of course. But *Intercom* is a far-flung enter-prise, not a parish magazine." He had suddenly started to speak English. It was strongly accented, but the intonation was English-English, not North American.

"Nevertheless—" I went into English too—"we are always interested in our correspondents' views and suggestions. They are often of great value to us. I take it, sir, that you are in Geneva on business."

He nodded vaguely. "Yes, business." He was peer-ing over my shoulder at the bookshelves now.

"Would you mind telling me how you came to hear about *Intercom?*"

I had his wandering attention again. "Not at all, Mr. Carter. I have a friend who subscribes." His smile sweetened. "However, since I was careless enough to lose one issue that he gave me to read he has become an unwilling lender. So, you gain a subscriber."

"And you retain a friend. I see." I made a mental note to check on other subscribers in the Hamburg area. "Of course, we have always known that many copies of *Intercom* are read by more than one person," I said. "We are glad that they are. We have never been interested in big circulations. Influence, in our case, is measured in terms of quality, not quantity."

It sounded phony to me even as I said it. I might have been an advertisement space salesman from some new shiny paper magazine venture trying to gouge a little action out of Rolls-Royce. I saw his eyebrows go up.

"But we like to know these things," I added lamely.

"And understandably." His hands spread out over my desk in a kind of benediction. "You are performing an invaluable public service and so are always on the alert for ways of enlarging and extending it."

It was said far too solemnly. For a moment I had a nasty suspicion that he was putting me on. Still, I could only play it straight.

"Just so," I said.

He leaned forward intently. "May I ask you a question, Mr. Carter?"

"By all means."

"Have you ever been threatened?"

"Our American attorneys have been kept quite busy from time to time."

He shook his head. "I was not thinking of legal action, Mr. Carter. After all, *Intercom*'s persistent questing after truth must have made it powerful enemies, enemies who would stop at nothing to silence it." The regretful smile was still in place but the eyes were wide and anxious. I decided that I

had been wrong about his trying to put me on. He
was just another nut like the rest of *Intercom*'s fans.

Still, he was entitled to value for his money. I
gave him the stern, no-nonsense editor look.

"Mr. Siepen, anyone who came here making
threats or looking for any other sort of trouble would
be out of luck."

"But what would you *do?*"

"That would depend on the circumstances."

"Let us say that you are approached by someone
who demands to know the source of some information you have published. What would be your attitude?"

"We never reveal sources. I'd tell him to go to
hell."

"You have a pistol?"

"No, I don't have a pistol." This one, I thought,
was really wacky.

"Suppose there is pressure, a threat of personal
violence perhaps."

"It hasn't come to that yet, Mr. Siepen."

"But if it should come, Mr. Carter, how would
you respond?"

He was looking at me very earnestly now. He
really wanted to know. I suddenly had the feeling
that this was some sort of test question for him, so
I thought before I answered. *Intercom* was supposed to be as tough on pacifism as it was on communism, and I didn't want this idiot reporting back
to Bloch's arms-dealing pals that I was unreliable.
On the other hand I wasn't prepared to talk the
bombastic he-man nonsense that I assumed he
wanted to hear. I know my limitations; in the he-
man area I am just not convincing. I tried laughing
the question off.

"That would depend on who is applying the
pressure or making the threat, Mr. Siepen. If he
were smaller than I am I might try throwing him
out myself. Otherwise I dare say I'd get the concierge up to help."

He was not amused. "Do you not feel, Mr. Carter, that violence or threats of violence are best dealt with by those whose business it is?"

"You mean by armies and police forces? Certainly."

His pals couldn't object to that, I thought; but he hadn't finished with me yet, he still hadn't made his point.

"Then the threatened or pressured person should call for help?"

"Obviously he should, if he needs it."

"And if he is in no position to call for help or if no help is available, what then? What then does he do?"

I was tired of this fooling around by then. "Mr. Siepen," I said, "I'm not very good with hypothetical questions. You tell *me* what he does."

He really smiled then, and I noticed that he had had bridgework done on the left upper jaw. "Mr. Carter," he said, "the man of sense submits to the pressure with good grace and does as he is told. As a man of sense yourself, would you not agree?"

How do you reply to that? Start talking about Galileo, or stand to attention and give him Henley's "Invictus"? Luckily I didn't have to reply because Nicole came back then with his receipt and change. He immediately got up and left. He just said goodbye. He didn't wait to hear whether I agreed with him or not.

"I'll tell you what I thought then, Mr. L. I thought that I'd been at the wrong end of a sounding-out and softening-up process. In that I think I was right. Where I got it wrong was in concluding that the pressures to which the man of sense was going to be subjected and to which he should, with good grace, submit would be coming from Mr. Siepen's direction. An understandable error, in my opinion.

Mr. L, I think that I met Colonel Jost before you did.

61

I think that "Mr. Siepen" was Colonel Jost and that the bastard stopped by that day just to let me know in advance that I couldn't win and, for his own comfort and convenience, to leave me with the thought that it would be better not to try.

So, my physical description of "Mr. Siepen" tallies with that of Colonel Jost.

Thank you, Mr. L, for letting me know. Your congratulatory pat on the head is also appreciated, although I must say that I find your contention that the gallant Colonel's visit to me was "a kindly gesture of concern" for my welfare on his part hard to stomach. As I see it, that gesture was about as kindly as the slap on the rump the lamb gets from the farmer when it's being loaded into the truck for the slaughterhouse. All Colonel Jost was interested in—if you've got your facts right, that is—was in seeing that his "part of the operation" ran smoothly and quickly. The attempt to soften me up in advance was just a little oil in the works. You say that he took "a certain risk" in coming to my office. What risk, for God's sake? Even supposing that one of the bogey-men had come to me later with a photograph of him—none of them ever did, of course, but let's suppose—and asked if I recognized the face, what could I have said to compromise him? "Yes, I've seen that man. He took out a subscription under the name of Siepen." So what? They know he's Jost, but what does that prove? Just that there's one more secret-service bigwig who didn't like *Intercom* and that this one gave it the personal once-over.

Kindly gesture, my foot!

On November 4, Dr. Bruchner called to tell me that the executors had accepted Arnold Bloch's offer for the *Intercom* shares. Because the executors were in America, he said, the legal transfer would take some days to complete, but I could now proceed as if it were an accomplished fact. In due course, no doubt, Herr Bloch would be communicating with me directly.

That was on a Friday. The first communication from Arnold Bloch was a letter which arrived the following Tuesday. It was written in English on his Munich office paper, but airmailed, I happened to notice, from Brussels. It was addressed to me personally at the *Intercom* office and was set out in the form of a memorandum.

> TO: *Theodore Carter, Geneva*
> FROM: *Arnold Bloch, Munich*
> SUBJECT: *"Intercom" editorial policy*

CONFIDENTIAL

You will have been advised by the Director of Intercom Publishing Enterprises A.G., Dr. Martin Bruchner of Bâle, of my organisation's acquisition of a controlling interest in the publication Intercom Newsletter.

The character of this publication is already well known to me and my associates, and Dr. Bruchner has informed you that no changes in its present character and editorial aims are either contemplated or desired. This decision I confirm.

We will, however, from time to time be furnishing you with items of news and information for inclusion in the publication. Such items will in all cases be of a type entirely suitable for inclusion, and will consist of technical bulletins likely to be of special interest to readers employed in government service. These bulletins will generally be brief and it is particularly requested that they are published exactly as they are received by you without elaboration or comment. Their predominantly technical character makes it necessary for us to insist upon this point.

As a conscientious editor you must naturally be at all times concerned that the material you publish is authentic. Special information bulletins coming from me or from my associates may be communicated to you by mail, telegram, Telex and, on occasion, telephone. In order that their source may in all cases be authenticated to you personally, and so accepted by you with complete confidence for immediate publication, the code designation SESAME *will precede all such bulletins. If the code designation* SESAME *is absent, this will mean that the bulletin is not authentic and that it should therefore be ignored.*

No acknowledgement of SESAME *bulletins need be made. Bulletins arriving too late for inclusion in the issue of the newsletter normally airmailed on Tuesdays should be included in the issue of the following week. Any questions arising out of the receipt or publication of* SESAME *bulletins should be addressed to me personally by telegram, though if the procedure outlined here is carefully followed such a necessity is unlikely to arise.*

A final word concerning your own position. I am glad to confirm formally your tenure of the post of Managing Editor pro tem of this publication. However, in the near future I and my associates may wish to discuss with you the possibility of changing the title of your post to that of "Managing Editor and Publisher." At that time, it is thought that a discussion of the corporation's financial arrangements with you and the possibility of their improvement at an early date may also be appropriate.

A brief acknowledgement by telegram of this memorandum would be appreciated.

It was signed *Bloch*.

When I say that this memorandum made me feel uneasy I am not indulging in hindsight.

I knew one thing for certain. The only way to keep *Intercom* afloat without a total subsidy was to see that it continued to be pretty outrageous and, above all, lively. The vision, which the memorancum conjured up, of commercial plugs by the dozen pouring in by mail, telegram and Telex was a depressing one. The promise that they would generally be brief I just couldn't believe. In my experience businessmen with things to sell can almost never bring themselves to be brief. Unless these "technical bulletins" were going to be written by professional admen, an unlikely prospect, they were bound, I thought, to be long-winded and dull. With much of that sort of stuff to carry, *Intercom* would soon be about as outrageous and lively as a mail-order catalogue.

The "code designation" SESAME thing bothered me for a different reason. Not only did it seem to me to be a piece of childish hanky-panky—"open Sesame" and the treasure house is revealed—it also suggested that Mr. Bloch and his associates took themselves and their investment so seriously that they feared that their competitors might try to muscle in on the act by sending in technical bulletins of their own. That argued delusions of grandeur. It also implied that they were counting on their *Intercom* promotion campaign to produce business results on a really important scale. Which meant in turn that if their grandiose expectations were to be disappointed—and I thought they probably would be —I could say goodbye to subsidies and my job.

The bit at the end about my new title and the improved financial arrangements only made me laugh. "Be a good boy and you may get another cooky." Even for a public-relations consultant, that, I thought, was a trifle crude.

I was right to be uneasy. I just picked the wrong

reasons for uneasiness and assigned them the wrong priorities.

I sent a brief telegram acknowledging the memorandum. "Received and understood," I said.

Only the first part of that statement can now be considered true.

Two days later I received, by mail postmarked Bonn, on Bloch's Munich paper, the first SESAME bulletin.

It was anything but brief. It was also, as I had expected, dreary.

You can look all this up in the *Intercom* file, Mr. L, but I remember that it started something like this:

Inquiries have been received recently about the assembly completion date of the new NATO FG115 fighter-reconnaissance aircraft. We are now able to inform our readers that test flights of the first assembled aircraft were carried out in Belgium two months ago during the week ending September 14. The speeds attained during these tests are, of course, classified "NATO SECRET," but on reliable authority we are able to say that they were in the vicinity of Mach 2.2. This was regarded as disappointing, as the prototypes attained the design speed of Mach 2.5. Difficulty was also experienced with the extremely high take-off speed at full load, and instability of the aircraft at subsonic speeds. Serious delays in delivery of the FG115 are regarded as certain.

If he had left it there it wouldn't have been too bad, though I itched to do a rewrite job on it; but he then went on to list the contractors involved in the manufacture of the plane. I don't mean just the air-frame and engine people, but *all* the contractors *and* subcontractors—undercarriage, hydraulics, automatic control equipment, fuel system, parachute braking release, ejection modules, the lot—with full names, head-office addresses and the locations of their plants. That bulletin took up a whole page single-spaced.

I assumed, naturally, that it was a smear job hashed up to discredit one or another of his clients' competitors. It went out in the *Intercom* issue dated November 15. That was the day the second SESAME bulletin arrived—too late for inclusion that week, so held over, as per instructions, until the following week.

The second bulletin was barely comprehensible, at least to me. It was a chatty little item about Soviet rocket fuels and at least half of it was taken up with chemical symbols set out in complicated diagrammatic arrangements. Ask Nicole about it. She had a terrible time cutting the stencils on that one and had to put in a lot of the lines by hand.

The general idea of it seemed to be that Soviet Army tactical nuclear missile units were reported to be in trouble because of the deterioration of certain missile fuels in storage. Red Army scientists were having a hard time solving the problem. The types of missile affected were given and the quantities thought to be involved. The chemical nature of the problem was described. With diagrams the bulletin took up a page and a half.

Aside from its length, total unreadability and the fact that I couldn't figure out the public-relations angle intended, what bothered me about that one was the policy question it raised. In the General's day the only kind of Soviet difficulties we had played up had been the political ones—China, revisionism, trouble with satellites, Ukrainian nationalism, stuff like that. The idea that Soviet missiles might not always be 100 per cent efficient would not have appealed to the General. If bugs had been found in *our* missiles, that would have been fine with him; that would have meant that there was treachery afoot and a conspiracy to expose;

but word of bugs in Soviet missiles would merely have served to encourage a slackening in the anti-communist Free World effort and to play into the hands of liberals, coexisters and pseudointellectuals. In the General's day I would have killed the story automatically without reference to him. Now, despite Herr Bloch's assurances, the character of *Intercom* was being made to change. There were a good many subscribers who still thought the way the General had. If they could understand what that bulletin was about I didn't think they would like it. I would get stern letters warning of the dangers of underrating a ruthless opponent and even hinting that we have been taken in by a cunning Soviet propaganda trick. That sort of thing was always bad for subscription renewals.

The third SESAME bulletin seemed relatively harmless. It was headed "Operation Triangle," though it didn't say what that was. It began by reporting a recent order, placed with an Italian firm by an American defence procurement agency in Brussels, for prefabricated concrete structures "of a new and interesting type." The question now, it went on, was to decide who would supply the "sensitive equipment" which had been designed to go inside these structures. There were many possibilities— here followed another ghastly list of names, addresses and plant locations—of which two (names again and presumably these were Bloch associates) were favoured by the scientific advisers on Operation Triangle.

We published that in the issue dated November 29.

Four days later another of the technical block-busters arrived. The envelope it came in was post-marked Copenhagen.

This bulletin was a detailed description of a new portable seismograph "constructed on the variable reluctance principle." It had been designed by a professor of physics in a Soviet university (name and address supplied) for the detection of low-yield underground atomic explosions at ranges up to five thousand kilometers. It was on the Soviet General Staff secret list.

The technical description itself was gibberish to me. The only thing that I could understand in that bulletin, apart from the preamble, was a footnote. This said that the technical information had been supplied by N. V. Skriabin, a member of the Soviet trade mission in Oslo.

That footnote really made me jump. Up to that point I had been prepared to take Herr Bloch more or less at his face value. Two of the bulletins so far published had been easily construable as attempts to influence government defence contract awards, in one way or another, for the benefit of his associates. The rocket-fuel story was more difficult to place, but I was prepared to attribute the difficulty to my ignorance of the subject matter and background. Talking about technical problems with Soviet rocket fuels *could* have been a subtle way of drawing attention to the existence of similar problems with our own. It was conceivable that one of Bloch's associates or clients had specialised know-how to sell and that this was the round-about way Bloch had chosen to interest the concerned parties in his man.

With Bulletin Four, however, no such possibility existed. All that Bloch was trying to do in that one, it seemed to me, was a hatchet job on Comrade Skriabin.

I thought about it a bit and then decided to wire for confirmation. This was the telegram I sent to Munich:

SESAME BULLETIN FOUR. IN LINE ESTAB-
LISHED INTERCOM POLICY QUESTION ADVIS-
ABILITY OF REVEALING SOURCE OF INFORMA-
TION AS GIVEN YOUR TEXT. PLEASE ADVISE.

For forty-eight hours I heard nothing. Then a telegram arrived from Brussels.

SESAME BULLETIN FOUR PUBLISH COMPLETE
AS RECEIVED.

So I did as I was told.

But from that moment on I disliked Herr Bloch. My sympathies were with N. V. Skriabin. It seemed to me that he had been put on the wrong end of a very dirty deal.

It wasn't long before I began to suspect that I might be in the same position.

Tuesdays, when we went to press, were noisy, with the Addressograph and mimeo machines going and the part-time help who came in to do the collating, folding and enclosing all chattering away at the tops of their voices; but Monday was my really busy day. That was when I put *Intercom* to bed. On Mondays I rarely left the office much before ten.

In the mornings I used to park my car in a side street near the church of St. Gervais and then walk across the river to the office. There was no easy parking nearer. By ten at night, though, the bridge I used to walk back over the river wasn't carrying much traffic and the streets beyond it were quiet, almost deserted.

I don't know when the surveillance began or which lot started it, but it was on a Monday night— Monday, December 5, just six days after the publication of SESAME Bulletin Four—that I first realised I was being followed.

FOUR

VALERIE CARTER
(transcribed tape interview)

I remember that night well.

My father came home, poured himself a whisky as usual and then forgot to drink it.

On those nights when he stayed late at the office I used to have hot soup ready for him, a sort of *pot au feu* with plenty of the vegetables he liked in it. When I brought the soup out of the kitchen that night I saw that his drink was still on the side table. He was at the window staring down at the street.

"I feel like Comrade Skriabin," he said.

I didn't know what he was talking about, so I just told him to eat the soup while it was hot.

He came over to the table and sat down. Then he looked up and gave me one of his small apologetic smiles. "Unless I'm completely off my head," he said, "I think that I was followed when I left the office tonight. Two men in a Fiat One-Two-Five. I think they're still outside. See if you can spot them, will you, Val?"

Now I know my father is sometimes silly, mostly when he's been drinking; but he's anything but stupid and certainly not fanciful. I'm not saying that he isn't neurotic, Mr. Latimer. For instance, this thing he has about calling you Mr. L. That's defensive. He thinks that if he calls you by your whole name that will somehow give you an advantage over him. He's done that with other people he's envied. Oh yes, I'm sure he envies you. He admires your books for one thing. You see, I love my father, but I don't think I have many illusions about him. He's a kind, clever, unhappy man who can be funny and delightful one moment and unbelievably awful the next. But even when he's awful he's still sane. He may have a vivid imagination, but he doesn't see things that don't exist.

So I went to the window and looked into the street.

Our apartment is on the third floor, as you know, but you can't see all the street below unless you open a window and lean out. It was a cold night and I didn't want to do that, so I just pressed my nose against the glass.

I could see enough. There *was* a Fiat parked a little way along across the street. That wasn't re-remarkable, of course; there were other cars parked there, too, most of them belonging to people in the apartments opposite. I could just see a bit of the roof of my father's Renault, which was parked directly below near our porte-cochère. As I looked down, I saw a man walk by the Renault and cross the street going towards the Fiat. He was wearing a felt hat and a dark overcoat. I couldn't see his face, naturally, but I noticed that although he appeared to walk slowly he took very long strides. When he reached the Fiat he opened the door on the passenger side and got in. With the opening of the door the interior light went on for a moment and I caught a glimpse of the gloved hands of a man in the driver's seat. Then the engine started and the headlights were switched on.

"They're going," I said and told him what I had seen.

My father went on with his supper. "Can you get the number?" he asked.

The Fiat was moving away now. "No, but I think it's a Fribourg plate."

"That's the one," he said.

I went over and sat down facing him.

"How do you know they were following you?" I asked.

"Pure chance." He shrugged. "I happened to notice that car when I left the office because it was illegally parked outside the bank on the corner. I thought of the long walk I had to reach my car, and in an uncharitable moment hoped that a policeman would come along and give the fellow a ticket. There was no policeman around, of course, but I kept on hoping. As I walked away I could still see him, you see, reflected in the shop windows. Then, just as I turned the corner, I saw his passenger get out and start walking the way I was going."

He broke a piece of bread and ate some more of the soup.

"I didn't think any more about it until I was walking across the bridge. Then that same car with the Fribourg plates passed me going north, the way I was going. Travelling quite fast he was. But not for long. As I turned off up the hill to St. Gervais I saw that he'd parked again. He didn't get out, just sat there. That made me think of the passenger he'd dropped and wonder which way *he'd* gone. You see I was getting curious about this fellow by then. When I reached my car I didn't start up immediately. Instead, I looked in the rear-view mirror. What I saw was interesting. I'd just walked along that stretch of road and none of the cars left there had had lights on. Now there *was* one with lights on. I couldn't be sure that it was the Fiat, of course—it was just two lights. But then a man came from the sidewalk and got in beside the driver. That I saw clearly."

"Because the interior light went on when the door opened?"

"That's right. How did you guess?"

"Because the same thing happened before they drove off just now."

"They were behind me all the way home," he said. "I thought at one moment of making a detour to see if they really were following me or if I was only imagining it, but I didn't."

"Why not?"

"Well, I knew that I *wasn't* imagining it." He smiled faintly. "Besides, if I'd started making detours they'd have known I'd spotted them. You know, if it hadn't been for that illegal parking outside the bank I *wouldn't* have spotted them, I wouldn't have noticed a thing."

"But why? And who could they be?"

"That's what I've been trying to figure." He got up and retrieved his drink from the side table. "I've got this far. Someone wants to know where I live. I'm not in the phone directory at this address, so I'm followed when I leave the office. When I lock my car and enter this building they wait a few minutes outside, then one of them comes across and checks the names on the mailboxes. Mission accomplished, they leave." He downed the drink. "Who are they? What do they want? I haven't a clue. It can't be the police or anyone connected with them. I'm registered at the Bureau des Etrangers. The police know where I live and all about me." He pushed his empty glass across. "Freshen it up for me, will you, Val?"

"All right." He was obviously very tired and I always tried to get him to go to bed early when he'd been working late. In the ordinary way I would have cleared the table then, washed the dishes, said good night and gone to my room. He usually went to his own soon after. But that night I didn't think he would. When he had things on his mind he was more likely to stay up and go on drinking.

I, too, had things on my mind.

I poured another drink and took it over to him. "Who is Comrade Skriabin?" I asked.

That was when he told me about the SESAME bulletins.

I had always hated *Intercom*. Writing that poisonous nonsense week after week, month in, month out, did something to my father. Oh, I know he didn't believe a word of what he wrote and that it was all done tongue in cheek. That was the way he excused it to himself. He would sometimes argue, too, that what he was doing for that old horror Novak was no worse than playing Tartuffe for an audience of half-wits; but he never argued it with much conviction, not with me at any rate. The truth was that for him *Intercom* became a way of thumbing his nose at the world, and in the end he grew to enjoy it, but at the expense of his self-respect.

I was glad when the General died and it looked as though *Intercom* was finished. Naturally, I realised that my father might have a hard time finding another job. That was why I suggested the translation-bureau idea. I was sure that it could be made to work, and at least he would be his own master. It wasn't journalism, of course; but then neither was *Intercom* unless you were prepared to give the word a new degraded meaning. When he told me about this man in Munich who was prepared to buy *Intercom* and wanted it to go on as before, I felt sick.

But not as sick as I felt when he told me about the SESAME bulletins on the night he was followed. I had known from the first that, in their dealings with this Arnold Bloch person, Dr. Bruchner and my father had been guided by little more than wishful thinking. What I had *not* realised until then was that they really knew absolutely nothing about the man.

I didn't sleep well that night. Next day I took a

copy of the Skriabin bulletin with me to the university library and did some work on it.

The first thing to establish, it seemed to me, was the merit, or lack of it, of the technical description of the seismograph. If it consisted of serious, original information, then N. V. Skriabin was certainly in trouble; if, on the other hand, it was merely a pageful of pretentious rubbish, then the "hatchet job," as my father called it, wasn't going to do much damage to anyone.

I found out that "variable reluctance" was a magnetic phenomenon and that it had indeed been applied in the design of some types of seismographs or seismometers. Such designs were associated mainly with the name of an American seismologist, H. Benioff, and variable-reluctance instruments were widely used. They were not, however, normally regarded as portable. Their weight was usually in the region of two hundred kilograms. Since the instrument described in the bulletin had a weight of only seventy kilograms, and since the method used to achieve this reduction in weight was specified in detail, I concluded that the technical material could well be genuine. I was able to check up, too, on the Russian geophysicist who had been credited with the design. He was certainly genuine and highly respected.

With N. V. Skriabin I had more difficulty. There was nothing in the seismological literature about him.

That didn't surprise me. A member of a Soviet trade mission might well have technical knowledge, but he was unlikely to be a scientist of the kind whose name appears in the indices of scientific journals. He was clearly a specialist of some kind; but the Soviet government doesn't publish lists of their departmental personnel as freely as some other countries, and such lists as are available generally cover only the senior bureaucrats. I couldn't find him in any of the lists we had. As I didn't know

what his specialty was—it could have been anything from herring fishery to machine tools—I knew
that I would get no further on my own. If I wanted
a lead I would have to go to a diplomatic source.
In the end I called up a friend in the library of the
UN European office at the Palais des Nations and
told him a lie. I told him that we had had an
inquiry from a foreign consulate-general about N.V.
Skriabin of the Soviet trade mission in Oslo and
asked if he could help me.

"That's funny," he said; "we had an inquiry here
about that man a few days ago. Ours wasn't from
a consulate-general, though, it was from the coun-
sellor of a foreign embassy in Bern. Who is the
consul-general?"

This man in the UN library was, as I say, a
friend. In fact we'd been students together and one
year he'd taken me to concerts. It had been one of
those things for a while. Then we had found that we
were in basic disagreement—about Bartók or sex, I
can't remember which now—and had called it off.
We were still on good terms, though, and I very
nearly told him the truth; but then I thought that
I had better not.

"It was a confidential inquiry," I said.

He laughed. "Well, so was ours, but I suppose
there's no harm in my telling you how we replied.
I can remember most of it, I think. Skriabin, Niko-
lay Viktorovich, is fifty-eight and a graduate of the
Moscow Institute of History, Philosophy and Literature. He joined the Party in thirty-two and later
entered the Soviet diplomatic service. During the
Hitler war he served in the army. Security duties of
some kind. He has one order of Lenin, two orders
of the Red Banner and one order of Survorov,
second class. Something like that anyway. I may
have got the numbers wrong. In recent years he has
served, diplomatic service again, in Stockholm, the
Hague, Brussels and Copenhagen. His highest diplomatic rank has been that of First Secretary. His

appointment to the Oslo trade mission was made last year. Doesn't sound as if he's done very well lately, does it?"

"No."

"In fact with a record like that it's highly probable that he is no longer a diplomat and hasn't been one for years. The informed guess here is that he is an officer of the Foreign Directorate of the Soviet Committee of State Security, otherwise known as the Komitet Gosudarstvennoi Bezopastnosti, or KGB, and that this trade-mission appointment is just another cover. Judging from the decorations he has, his rank is probably equivalent to that of colonel. He'd be quite an important person, a resident director most likely."

"Oh."

"I wouldn't pass the KGB thought on to your consulate-general. Better let them work that one out for themselves."

"Yes. Thank you. I'm very grateful to you."

He asked me to have dinner later that week, and to get rid of him I agreed. I forgot about the dinner date, I'm afraid, because so many other things had begun happening by then. At the time, though, I just wanted to think about what he had told me.

You see, Mr. Latimer, it was all very confusing— confusing to me anyway. I had been sure from the start that my father had the wrong idea. He had decided that this man Skriabin was some poor, wretched underling who had been cajoled by Bloch into selling technical secrets and that Bloch, having got the secrets, had chosen to betray him through *Intercom* rather than pay him off. I couldn't see that. I mean, if you're getting technical or trade secrets from someone, secrets you hope to make money out of, you might cheat the person you got them from by informing on him to his employers, but you wouldn't publish the secrets as well. That would be silly. Now that I knew that Skriabin wasn't a poor, wretched underling, things were even sillier.

If you're Bloch the double-crossing promoter, you don't publish information of value to your competitors; and if you're Bloch the proud new owner of anti-communist *Intercom*, you certainly don't publish the name of a potential KGB defector so that the Russians can whisk him back to the Soviet Union before he gets away. So none of it made sense.

I couldn't make up my mind whether to tell my father what I had found out about N. V. Skriabin or not. I decided to wait and see what kind of a mood he was in.

The private researches I had been doing that day had put me behind with my normal work in the library, so I was late home. When I got there I found that we had guests. I saw their overcoats and hats lying on a chair in the hall when I opened the outer door.

I didn't go in immediately. It was rare for us to have unexpected guests—the Swiss prefer to order their social lives with a certain formality—so I concluded that these were foreigners. The overcoats and hats had no apparent nationality and the murmur of voices from the living room was indistinct, but there was an attaché case beside the coats that looked American, and one of those soft leather carrying bags that professional photographers use for their cameras. Both case and bag had Air France cabin baggage tags on the handles. Americans from Paris perhaps.

I had had a tiring day. I hoped to God that my father, inclined over drinks to become too hospitable, wouldn't invite them to stay to dinner. I went to my room and ran a comb through my hair before presenting myself.

One of them was tall, the other short. The short man was doing the talking when I went in.

"But isn't all this hard-line stuff a bit old hat these days?" he was saying. "I mean . . ."

Then he saw me, broke off and got to his feet.

79

He was a plump, hair-receding forty with a round fleshy face, an Edgar Allan Poe moustache and heavily lidded eyes. His complexion was what my father would call flounder-belly beige. He wore a dark business suit and a Charvet tie the colour of squashed beetroot. He cocked his head slightly and gave me a toothy smile.

When my father turned towards me I saw that he had his suppressed white-rage look. That was some comfort. I knew at once that these particular guests would not be asked to stay to dinner. On the other hand, he was quite capable of plying them with more drinks simply in order to keep them there until he had decided which would be the most wounding method of insulting them.

He made a ceremony of the introductions.

"Ah, Val dear—" he kissed me lightly on the cheek, a thing he never does when we are alone— "this is Mr. Goodman. His accomplice in crime, there—" he pointed his glass at the tall man gangling awkwardly by the sofa—"is Mr. Rich. Gentlemen, my daughter Valerie."

I received an *"Enchanté, Mademoiselle"* from Mr. Goodman and a baritone "Miss Carter" from the accomplice.

I said, "Good evening."

"Mr. Goodman and Mr. Rich are Americans," my father went on, "and they have come all the way from the Paris bureau of *World Reporter* magazine. They are making a study—I beg their pardon, an In-Depth Study—" his tone supplied derisory capitals—"of the international personalized intelligence services. And they actually believe that I may be able to help them. So they are interviewing me. Or rather Mr. Goodman is interviewing me, while Mr. Rich, the photographer of the party, fingers his camera hopefully and looks for openings. Isn't that exciting, my dear?"

He made it sound as if they were assaulting him.

"Very exciting," I said. "I'll leave you to it."

"No, no, Val." He pressed me into a chair. "I'd like you to stay. Mr. Rich would, too, I can see. You are so much prettier to look at than I am, and he is after all a photographer, an artist. Eh, Mr. Rich? As for Mr. Goodman, I'm sure he won't mind an addition to his audience."

"Delighted," said Mr. Goodman.

"Yes." My father gave him a grim smile. "Mr. Goodman plumbing the depths of his subject is really worth listening to. As long, that is, as you remember that depth is a relative term and that our Mr. Goodman takes his soundings with nothing longer than a chewed toothpick." He spat out the last two words quite venomously.

Mr. Goodman chuckled and glanced at Mr. Rich. "See what I mean," he said. "I told you. There's no mistaking Theo Carter's style. Trenchant, hard-hitting, with club in one hand and rapier in the other—pure *Intercom*. He writes it all. Always has done. Every word. Isn't that right, Miss Carter?"

"I thought that it was my father you were interviewing." I went across to the side table and poured myself a glass of Dézaley.

He ignored me from then on.

"How about it, Theo? The whole letter is your work, right?"

"I edit it, yes."

"That wasn't quite what I asked, but never mind. Let's go back to the General for a moment. Did he okay every story that went in?"

"Of course not. There was an editorial policy. I carried that policy out, applied it. I still do."

"I want to come to that. Just let's get just this thing clear. The policy was always hard-line anti-communist. Right?"

"Right."

"And hard-line anti-Administration, too, eh?"

"You know the General's history as well as I do."

"Anti-Administration, is that your answer?"

"Yes."

"But never anti-American?"

"You asked me that before. You're repeating yourself, Mr. Goodman."

"Tell me again, Theo."

I had thought at first that what had so annoyed my father was Mr. Goodman's calling him "Theo"; now I saw that there was more to it than that; there was Mr. Goodman's hectoring manner. This was not just a journalist conducting an interview; this was an interrogator with a suspect, an inquisitor seeking out heresy.

I wondered what Mr. Rich thought of his companion's technique. He was sitting on the sofa, absently stroking the strobe light pack lying beside him. He had scarcely touched his drink. He was lean and quite good-looking in a nondescript way; older than Mr. Goodman clearly, but certainly a great deal healthier. There was a copy of *Réalités* on the table in front of him and he stared down at it, frowning slightly as if the cover design puzzled him. His attitude reminded me suddenly of a play reading I had attended a few days earlier; it had been of a new translation into French of the *Philoctetes* and I had noticed the translator sitting with his head down and frowning in the same way as he listened to the actors reading the lines.

"But there have been changes lately, haven't there, Theo?"

"Of ownership, yes. Of policy, no."

"Oh come *on,* Theo." Goodman's teeth were showing and his eyes had narrowed. "Come *on,* don't give me that."

My father stood up. "You asked me a question, Mr. Goodman. I gave you an answer. You're supposed to be a professional reporter. Why don't you behave like one?"

He came over to pour himself another drink. I was still standing by the side table and I could see that he was trembling. There was nothing suppressed about his anger now. I took the glass from his hand.

"I'll do it."

"Thank you, Val. Just one," he added distinctly; "these people will be leaving in a minute."

Goodman gave a little whistle. "Now that's not very friendly, Theo. We've only just started."

My father walked back to him. "*You* may have just started, but I'm just about through," he said. "You invited yourself here. Okay, so now I'm inviting you to get the hell out."

Goodman threw up his hands in mock amazement. "All I asked was a question." He appealed to Rich. "Did I say something I shouldn't?"

Rich shrugged. "Maybe Mr. Carter doesn't want to tell about his new owner," he said; "maybe he's under orders."

"Yeah, maybe." Goodman nodded gravely. "Is that it, Theo?"

"You haven't asked me about the new owner," my father retorted, "so why should you think I don't want to tell you about him?"

"That's true. Okay, let's talk about Arnold Bloch. Have I got that name right, Theo? B-l-o-c-h? That's how Dr. Bruchner gave it to us."

For some reason the mention of Dr. Bruchner seemed to shake my father. He sat down again.

"Yes, that's right," he said.

"And he's in Munich?"

"He has an office there."

"German?"

"He speaks German."

"Then he's German. Right?"

"Why don't you ask him?"

"We're asking you, Theo."

"I don't know. I've never met him."

"Ah-hah!" Goodman affected wide-eyed wonder. "Man of mystery, eh?"

"If you want to make him a man of mystery, go

ahead. As an industrial PR man he could probably use the publicity. Good for business."

"That's what he is, is he? A PR man?"

"I just said so. Aren't I speaking plainly?"

"We want to get it straight, Theo."

It had become "we" not "I" with Mr. Goodman now, I noticed. I gave my father his fresh drink. I had made it a strong one.

"So it's Bloch who's responsible for the new *Intercom* policy. That right?"

For a moment I thought that my father was going to throw the drink at him. If he had had anything other than a drink in his hand I think he would have thrown it. As it was he put the glass down carefully and waited before he spoke.

"For the last time," he said quietly, "and I mean for the *last* time, there is no new policy. Mr. Bloch likes *Intercom* the way it is, and he wants it to stay that way."

"Okay. So Arnold Bloch is an absentee landlord and you're the guy who's minding the store. Right, Theo?"

"Right."

"Then maybe we can get down to a couple of specifics." Goodman pulled a small notebook from his pocket and flicked it open. "On November fifteen you ran a story about the test flights of the new FG one-one-five fighter-reconnaissance plane and some teething troubles they were having with it."

"Yes."

"Was that in line with *Intercom* editorial policy?"

"It was."

"Handing NATO troubles to the Russians on a plate?"

"No. Exposing inefficiency and negligence so that a potential weakness isn't allowed to become a real and present danger."

"I see."

And then my father made a mistake. "Anything anti-American about that?" he asked.

"Ah then, you *do* see the point, Theo."

"What point?"

"The point of our asking about this particular story. No, there's nothing anti-American or un-American about exposing inefficiency and negligence. We do it all the time, don't we? But do we also give aid and comfort to the enemy by supplying him with chapter and verse in the shape of a list of contractors and subcontractors on the secret list? No sir, we do not. Not if we're still the old *Intercom,* known and loved by every crackpot in the Congress. Let's move on, Theo." He flicked another page of the notebook. "November twenty-two. Story about trouble with Soviet rocket missile fuels. What was your angle on that one?"

I knew that he was talking about the second SESAME bulletin now and my heart was in my mouth; but my father almost smiled as he answered. He didn't even seem angry any more.

"Wasn't it obvious?" he said. "Bad news for their side is good news for ours. We're entitled to some encouragement, I think."

"Did you write that story, Theo?"

"No, I did not."

"But you said you always wrote the whole newsletter."

"No, Mr. Goodman. *I* didn't say that, *you* said it. I said that I *edited* the newsletter."

"Then who *did* write that story, Theo? Where did you get it?"

My father got to his feet. "All right, Mr. Goodman," he said, "the ball game's over. I'd like to be charitable. You could be too stupid or ignorant to know that you can't ask a question like that and expect to get a responsive answer. But though I know you're stupid, I'm damned certain you're not ignorant. So from now on all the answers are going to be the same—no comment, get out."

Goodman smiled. "Cool it, Theo. No need for the editorial high horse. I'll put the question another way."

"If my daughter weren't here I'd tell you *where* you could put the question. *How* you put it doesn't interest me. The answer is still no comment. Now get out. Both of you."

There was a silence. It was Rich who moved first. He got to his feet, picked up his camera and put the carrying strap of the strobe light pack over his shoulder.

My father watched him with a sardonic smile. "Know how to work that thing?" he asked.

Rich did not answer for a moment; then he said, "Thanks for the drink, Mr. Carter" and walked out into the hall.

To my surprise Goodman immediately rose and, without even a glance at my father, followed

I hesitated, then went after them. Rich already had his overcoat on and was putting the camera in the carrying bag. I went past them and opened the front door.

Goodman was ready first. "Good night, Miss Carter," he said. "Pleasure meeting you."

It hadn't been a pleasure meeting him, so I said nothing. In any case he was already on his way down the stairs.

Rich's departure was slower. "Thanks," he said; "we could have seen ourselves out." But then, in the doorway, he paused and said something else.

"Tell your father to be careful, Miss Carter."

"Of what, Mr. Rich?"

He shrugged. "It's an unhealthy world and there are some people in it who never take 'no comment' for an answer. Tell him that. Good night, Miss Carter."

He was gone then. I shut the door and went back to the living room.

My father was pouring himself another drink.

"That photographer just said . . ." I began.

He cut me short. "I know. I heard. And he's no more a photographer than I am."

"What is he then?"

"Wasn't it obvious? Central Intelligence Agency. One of the CIA's golden boys. A spook. A bogey-man. It stuck out a mile. Bloody impertinence."

"Was that why you asked him if he knew how to work a camera? I thought you were just being rude."

"Rude? You call that rude? What about them? The oldest gag in the world and they thought they could pull it on me. And with a punk like Goodman to front for them. It's insulting."

"You mean that Mr. Goodman *isn't* from the *World Reporter* magazine?"

"No, of course I don't mean that. He's on the magazine all right. They wouldn't be *that* clumsy. No need to be anyway. Lots of the newsmen string along with the CIA and do little chores for them. But Goodman! And a photographer for Pete's sake! Gossip-column stuff. Whoever heard of an in-depth interview by a news-magazine reporter being conducted with a photographer present? Even Goodman knew how fishy that was. When he called me at the office he didn't mention any photographer."

"Did he know your home address?" I asked.

That gave him pause. "Oh," he said, "I see. You're thinking about that business last night. Let me think. No. What Goodman wanted was to come to the office. I told him that it was press day and that we wouldn't be able to hear ourselves speak. I suggested he come here and gave him the address. I thought then that it was going to be a more sociable occasion."

"So all we need to know now is why the Central Intelligence Agency suddenly wants to ask you questions. Has it ever happened before?"

"No. They've been mad at us plenty of times, of course. But that's always been because we've made

what they called 'unnecessary work' for them, checking out the bees in the General's bonnet. This is
different."

"We still need to know why."

He sat down wearily. "Okay, Val. No need to
push it. I'm not stupid. We know why."

"The SESAME bulletins?"

"What else?"

So then I told him what I had found out about
N. V. Skriabin.

When I had finished he said "Oh, God" and
reached for more whisky.

I went into the kitchen. It was too late by then
to cook properly, so I started reheating the *pot au
feu*. After a bit my father came in and stood watching me while I chopped vegetables to add to the
soup.

He was a little drunk by then, as I'd known he
would be—not silly drunk, but prepared to be
whimsical.

I didn't mind. That night I felt like getting drunk
myself. He leaned against the refrigerator.

"You know what, Val?" he said. "You know what
we're doing?"

"No."

"Well, most people, people like Goodman for
example, when they have a problem they make an
in-depth study of it. Right?"

"Right." I had heard the word too much that
evening and was beginning to dislike it.

"Right," he said. "Now we're different. We've
got a problem. But do we make an in-depth study
of it? We do not. With us it's an *out-of-depth*
study." He paused. "And just for laughs," he added
slowly, "there's another SESAME bulletin in the issue
that went out today."

I didn't answer. I couldn't.

My father went away then and a few moments
later I heard him fumbling with the door of the
bathroom.

Part Two

Sellers' Market

FIVE

NARRATIVE RECONSTRUCTION
December 12 to 16

Theodore Carter's assessment of his position on the night of December 13 was an accurate one. He was indeed out of his depth.

By the end of that week so was Dr. Bruchner. By then, he too had received strange callers and been involved in disturbing conversations.

Advokaturbureau Rungholt & Winkler in Bâle is an old established firm. There are now eight partners and most of their practice is concerned with tax and corporation law. On the list of partners Dr. Bruchner ranks fourth.

He remembers being interviewed by Goodman and Rich on December 12 mainly because they arrived at his office without having first written or telephoned for an appointment. He agreed to receive them only when they pleaded that they had travelled from Paris expressly to see him.

The interview was brief. As soon as Goodman's line of questioning became apparent, Dr. Bruchner headed him off by explaining that his connection with Intercom Publishing Enterprises A.G. was purely legal and fiscal and that *Intercom's* editorial policies were not his concern. He referred them to Carter. In response to further questions he did, however, tell them of Arnold Bloch's existence and his ownership of the shares. There had been no reason to conceal facts which were matters of public record in the Zug Register of Commerce. He practiced only one minor deception on them. He allowed them to assume that his refusal to give them any further information about Herr Bloch was motivated by professional discretion. His reticence was understandable. Dr. Bruchner was already finding his ignorance on the subject of Herr Bloch a trifle absurd and he was reluctant to parade it unnecessarily. When Goodman said that they might later decide to interview Arnold Bloch personally, Dr. Bruchner thought that a good idea and wished them well. After they had gone he told his secretary to buy the international edition of *World Reporter* for the next few weeks and check it for references to *Intercom*.

During the morning of December 14 he received a telephone call, from Theodore Carter. That was the morning after Goodman and Rich had been to Carter's apartment.

Carter was in an excited state and at times barely coherent. He wanted to know how he could get in touch with Arnold Bloch. He said that the matter was vitally urgent but would not say why nor what it was that had to be discussed. When Dr. Bruchner gave him the Munich number, Carter said something in English about "taking the finger out" which Dr. Bruchner didn't quite understand, and then explained that he had been trying the Munich number for two hours without getting any reply. Dr. Bruchner had started to suggest that he send a telegram when Carter suddenly hung up.

Five hours later Dr. Bruchner himself was trying urgently to reach Arnold Bloch by telephone.

That was after his meeting with Dr. Schwob.

Bank Schwob of Bâle is a highly respectable concern. In Switzerland the *privatbankier* functions in much the same way as an investment banker or mutual-fund administrator in London or New York; he manages money for investors. The main dif-

92

ference between the Swiss private banker and his Anglo-Saxon counterpart is that the Swiss is not permitted by law to incorporate his bank and enjoy limited liability. He must back his judgment with his private fortune. Dr. Julius Schwob is a third-generation banker and his fortune is considerable. A sudden request for an early meeting from such a man would be flattering even to a lawyer of Dr. Bruchner's standing and experience. He promptly rearranged his appointments for that afternoon to accommodate the banker.

The meeting took place in Dr. Schwob's somewhat shabby second-floor office. Present, in addition to Drs. Schwob and Bruchner, was a procurator of the bank.

The procurator took notes. It was Dr. Schwob who did most of the talking.

"We have a client," he said, "who is interested in a foreign-owned company which you, Dr. Bruchner, direct."

Dr. Bruchner was director of a number of companies owned by foreigners, so he just nodded politely and waited.

"Intercom Publishing Enterprises A.G.," said Dr. Schwob.

The lawyer failed to repress the grunt of surprise that came to his throat.

Dr. Schwob interpreted the sound as an expression of disappointment. His deprecating shrug now made it plain that his client's interest was neither shared nor commended by Bank Schwob. "A small affair, I realise," he said, "and not one to which you devote a great deal of your valuable time. Nevertheless, to our client it is of some interest. May we know the present status of the majority shareholding formerly owned by your late client, the American, Novak?"

"Certainly. Early in November the shares were purchased from the Novak estate by Herr Arnold Bloch of Munich."

"Who still holds all of them?"

"Yes."

"Do you act for Herr Bloch?"

"I am not his personal attorney, but in the matter of this company I act upon his instructions and for his account."

"Then you could transmit an offer for the shares to him."

"I could, yes. Herr Bloch is, according to my understanding, acting in concert with certain French and West German associates."

"Is Herr Bloch an industrialist?"

"He is an industrial public-relations consultant."

"Still, I take it that his associates would not be averse to taking a profit on their investment if they were given the opportunity."

Dr. Bruchner thought before replying to that. The reasons Bloch had given him for wanting to buy *Intercom* had been convincing and he had accepted them. Bloch had planned to use it to channel publicity for his associates' products and services to persons who might influence the awarding of government contracts, and had been prepared to pay a good price for the shares on that account. Presumably he still planned to use it that way. It was possible—Dr. Bruchner did not know then about the SESAME memorandum to Carter, nor about the bulletins which had been published—that he was already doing so. In that case Bloch would not be interested in selling out for a paltry profit on a mere ten thousand dollars. Dr. Bruchner made up his mind.

"I am prepared to submit any offer you may care to make for the shares," he said; "but I think I should tell you that Herr Bloch and those he represents did not buy the *Intercom* company with the object or expectation of making a profit from its operations. Their object was to maintain and control an established information service which could on occasion be of indirect assistance to them in pursuing their other business activities. Herr Bloch and his associates are persons of substance. It is possible, of course, that they could be induced to sell, but in my opinion an offer for the shares would have to be substantial if it is to be an effective inducement."

Dr. Schwob looked down his nose. "They paid ten thousand dollars American for the shares," he said. "Would you consider an offer of fifty thousand substantial?"

"Fifty thousand francs?"

"Fifty thousand dollars American."

Dr. Bruchner kept his head very well. He did not allow his jaw to drop and successfully resisted an impulse to grin foolishly.

"I would consider that substantial, yes," he said. "Is that the offer you wish me to convey to Herr Bloch?"

"It is."

"Then may I have it in writing?"

"You may." Dr. Schwob motioned to the procurator, who produced a document from a folder he had been nursing. "However, I must point out that this is a conditional offer. It is good only for two days, until the close of business on Friday, that is. If it is not accepted by then it must be considered as withdrawn."

Dr. Bruchner had been thinking quickly. "I may not be able to get a decision by then," he said. "As I told you, Herr Bloch is not the only one concerned."

"He is the owner of the shares. If he wishes to consult his associates he can do so by telephone. We have no intention of allowing our offer to be used as a bargaining counter."

Dr. Bruchner was on the point of saying that an offer to buy cannot be used as a bargaining counter when there is only one bidder, but thought better of it. If Dr. Schwob really believed that there were others who might be prepared to pay outlandish prices for *Intercom* shares, this was no time to disillusion him. Dr. Bruchner wished dearly that it had been permissible for him to ask the name of Bank Schwob's free-spending client. Herr Bloch would undoubtedly want to know, too. But there was nothing to be done about that; to ask would be not only unthinkably indiscreet but also, since he would receive no answer, pointless.

So all he said was "Very well. I will do my best to reach Herr Bloch today. In any case I will get back to you by Friday."

He returned to his own office and set about getting in touch with Arnold Bloch.

There was no reply from the Munich number. Remembering the difficulty Carter had complained of that morning, Dr. Bruchner was not surprised. He drafted a telegram reporting the offer and the Friday deadline and requesting an immediate reply. He had that sent off to the Munich address; then, as an afterthought, he gave instructions for a copy of the telegram to be sent to Arnold Bloch in care of the Munich bank he had used when he had paid for the shares originally.

Thursday afternoon came and there was still no reply from Bloch. Dr. Bruchner's secretary tried telephoning the Munich number again, but again without result. She telephoned the Munich bank. The bank said that it could not give out information about its customers but would forward a letter if requested to do so.

By Friday morning Dr. Bruchner was worried. He had promised to give Dr. Schwob an answer before the bank closed that day, and it was beginning to look as if his answer would have to be a lame admission that he had been unable to contact his client. He could request an extension of time, no doubt, and perhaps get it; but that was not the way he liked to do business with men of Dr. Schwob's calibre.

He told his secretary to try the Munich number

yet again and to keep on trying it at hourly intervals.

At ten o'clock the number answered. Moments later the secretary spoke to Dr. Bruchner.

"The Munich number," she said breathlessly; "the police wish to speak to you."

"What police?"

"The Munich police, Herr Doktor. The police answered the telephone."

"Very well."

The man in Munich identified himself as a detective of the criminal police.

"You are Herr Bloch's lawyer?" he asked.

"I represent him here in Bâle. Why? What has happened?"

"That is what we are investigating, Herr Doktor. A cleaning woman reported to the building janitor this morning that Herr Bloch's offices had been broken into during the night. The janitor reported to us. I am in the office now. Do you know Herr Bloch's office here?"

"No."

"It is a small suite only, an outer and an inner office. There is a filing cabinet and a desk. These appear to have been searched. Herr Bloch is not in Munich at present, and the janitor has no knowledge of his whereabouts. We cannot tell whether anything is missing until Herr Bloch or someone representing him can make an inventory of the contents. Do you know where Herr Bloch can be found?"

"I thought he was in Munich. That is why I am telephoning his office. His bank has an address for him. They would no doubt give it in an emergency, if requested to do so by the police." He gave the name of the bank and his own name and number in Bâle. "If you reach Herr Bloch today," he added, "please ask him to contact me at once."

The detective said that he would do so.

Just after three o'clock that afternoon, while Dr. Bruchner was trying to decide how best to frame a request to Dr. Schwob for an extension of the deadline, a telegram from Arnold Bloch arrived:

> OFFER FROM BANK SCHWOB SHOULD BE REJECTED AS TOTALLY INADEQUATE. INFORM THEM OFFER IN DOLLARS U.S. OF HALF MILLION WOULD BE CONSIDERED AS MINIMUM BASIS FOR SERIOUS NEGOTIATION THOUGH DELAY PERMITTING COMPETITIVE OFFERS WOULD DOUBTLESS ESCALATE ACCEPTABLE FIGURE. ADVISE DEVELOPMENTS BY TELEGRAM POSTE RESTANTE 1065 BRUSSELS COPY TO MUNICH
> BLOCH

The telegram had been sent from Stuttgart.

Dr. Bruchner read it through twice, concluded that Arnold Bloch had taken leave of his senses and decided to disregard most of his instructions.

When he got through to Dr. Schwob he said only that Herr Bloch had rejected the offer.

"You mean that he does not wish to sell at any price?" demanded Dr. Schwob.

"No, he does not say that. He describes the offer you have made as inadequate."

"Has he given you any indication of what he would consider adequate?"

Dr. Bruchner began to sweat. He did not want to quote the astronomical asking price mentioned in Bloch's telegram for fear of being himself condemned as frivolous and irresponsible. He had his and his firm's conservative reputations to consider. On the other hand he was most reluctant to lie to Dr. Schwob. If the banker's client was prepared to pay fifty thousand dollars for shares with a nominal value of ten thousand, he obviously wanted them very badly, was perhaps determined to have them. It was conceivable that such a man, if thwarted, might decide to make a direct approach to Arnold Bloch. All parties would then learn that Dr. Bruchner had not only disobeyed a client's written instructions but also misrepresented them. He would stand convicted of unprofessional conduct. He tried to hedge.

"Herr Bloch indicates that he does not feel that your present offer could provide even a starting point for serious negotiation," he said. "He does not, I repeat, say that he will under no circumstances sell. But he is clearly unwilling to sell except at a price which I am afraid your client would find prohibitive." He floundered on hastily, away from that danger zone. "As I told you at our meeting the other day, *Intercom* has for Herr Bloch an indirect commercial value—indirect, distinct and quite unrelated to its face value as a going concern, and certainly much greater."

The last part of this speech had been accompanied by sounds of impatience from Dr. Schwob's end of the line. He broke in now.

"Evidently," he said, "our client had this indirect value, as you call it, in mind when he asked us to make this offer on his behalf. The figures speak for themselves."

For a moment Dr. Bruchner felt easier. If the banker and his client both accepted the fact that what they were bidding for so extravagantly was not just a decrepit little publishing company but a subsidiary asset of that company, an asset as intangible and as hard to evaluate as, say, good will, then the whole discussion suddenly became less unreal. The prospective buyer, Dr. Bruchner decided, was probably one of Arnold Bloch's business rivals.

His relief was short-lived. He had started to say something about the difficulty of arriving at a fair price in these cases when Dr. Schwob cut in peremptorily.

"How much?" he said.

Dr. Bruchner started to hem and haw.

"How much?" Dr. Schwob repeated sharply.

Dr. Bruchner still tried to postpone the evil moment. "Half a million," he mumbled.

But Dr. Schwob was merciless. "Francs?" he demanded.

There could be no further evasion. Dr. Bruchner took a deep breath. "No, dollars American," he said and waited for the sky to fall.

To his utter astonishment it didn't. There was a two-second silence and then Dr. Schwob said quietly: "A moment, please."

A longer silence. The banker was evidently thinking. Then he spoke again.

"There is no doubt about that figure, Dr. Bruchner? No possibility of error?"

"None. I received my instructions in writing from Herr Bloch."

"I see."

Emboldened, Dr. Bruchner conveyed the rest of his instructions. "I was to tell you also, Dr. Schwob, that the half million should be considered as a minimum price. Should delay in negotiating the sale give others time to put in higher bids, Herr Bloch would not feel bound to accept the half million. This is in no sense an exclusive offer to sell at an agreed price."

"I understand the position." Dr. Schwob's tone was calmly businesslike. "Naturally we will have to consult with our client. If he should decide to instruct us further in the matter we will let you know."

"Thank you." Dr. Bruchner had quite recovered now. "Would you like me to send you a letter confirming Herr Bloch's counter-offer?"

"I don't think that will be necessary." The banker paused as if about to end the conversation, but then went on. "Your client is a bold man, Dr. Bruchner."

"He seems to know his own mind, yes."

"And with that knowledge goes prudence, I trust."

Since he was privately of the opinion that his client was demented, Dr. Bruchner did not quite know how to reply to that. "I would very much hope so," he said awkwardly.

Dr. Schwob was suddenly jovial. "I would very much hope so too," he said. "Goodbye, Dr. Bruchner."

"Goodbye, Dr. Schwob."

Dr. Bruchner put down the telephone, wiped his forehead with his handkerchief and called for his secretary. To Herr Bloch in Brussels he sent the following telegram:

> BANK SCHWOB CONSIDERING YOUR TERMS. WILL
> KEEP YOU INFORMED DEVELOPMENTS IF ANY.
> REGRET MUNICH POLICE REPORT YOUR OFFICES
> THERE FORCIBLY ENTERED LAST NIGHT BY UN-
> KNOWN INTRUDERS. POLICE REQUEST EARLY
> PRESENCE YOU OR AUTHORISED REPRESENTA-
> TIVE IN ORDER DETERMINE PROPERTY MISSING.
> BRUCHNER

He thought next of Theodore Carter's anguished call earlier in the week and considered telephoning him to pass on Bloch's *poste restante* address in Brussels. Then he decided not to telephone. Two days had gone by without further word from Carter, so presumably his need to contact Bloch was no longer urgent. He knew that this was wishful thinking on his part; but with so much else on his mind concerning *Intercom* he did not want to hear about Carter's troubles just then. Carter could wait.

He called for the current *Intercom* back-number file.

Normally Dr. Bruchner did not trouble to read *Intercom*. His secretary disposed of the weekly issues as they arrived by inserting them in a loose-leaf box file. There was a file for each year and they were kept on a shelf in her office. In earlier days Dr. Bruchner had sometimes referred to them—usually in order to brief himself in preparation for a meeting with the General—but he had had no occasion to do so recently. As he had told Goodman, what went into *Intercom* was nothing to do with him. He managed the company's business affairs; the rest was in Theodore Carter's hands.

Now, however, things were different. Dr. Schwob's calm reception of Bloch's preposterous counter-offer had made the lawyer curious. By now, too, he was wondering how his own position would be affected if the company's shares were to change hands for a large sum of money. He had talked glibly about indirect values and subsidiary assets, but why had nobody seen before that they existed? While the General had been alive there had never been even so much as an inquiry about *Intercom* shares, much less an offer to buy them. Yet within three months of his death there had been two offers, first from Bloch—and he had paid more for the shares than they had then seemed to be worth—and now from Bank Schwob's client. What had happened to *Intercom*? Why had it suddenly become so desirable a property?

He began to read.

Dr. Bruchner is not only a trained lawyer. As an able-bodied adult Swiss male below the age of sixty, he is also a trained soldier. He is an army reserve major and his annual training that year had included attendance at a course on staff duties.

He had no difficulty in singling out the SESAME bulletins as likely Bloch contributions. It was obvious that they had not been written by Carter. However, the satisfaction he derived from the discovery that he could detect stylistic differences in English was short-lived. Although he was not sufficiently well informed to be able to identify the bulletins as NATO and Warsaw Pact classified intelligence leaks, he knew enough to find them collectively rather disturbing. Reviewing them in the context of his recent conversation with Dr. Schwob, he began to get worried. He had a suspicion that there was something going on with *Intercom* that he would rather not know about.

Better then, he wondered, not to inquire further? Better to leave it alone? He himself was, after all, acting in complete good faith, as no doubt was Dr. Schwob. They were merely trusted intermediaries between the prospective buyer and the prospective seller of a piece of corporate property. The motives of those principals were really not their concern, legally or morally.

However, Dr. Bruchner did like to leave his office for the day with a clear professional conscience, and that evening he chose to clear it by reversing a decision he had made earlier. He put in a call to Theodore Carter with the idea of giving him Bloch's *poste restante* address in Brussels.

There was no reply from the *Intercom* office— it was after six o'clock—so he put in a call to Carter's home number. There was no reply from that either. So Dr. Bruchner sent Carter a telegram giving him the address. In the circumstances, he felt, he had done his best to be helpful.

SIX

FROM THEODORE CARTER
(transcribed dictation tape)

The reason that Dr. Bruchner was unable to reach me by phone that Friday night was that I was in the process of being kidnapped at the time.

With that in mind, Mr. L, I know you won't be too disappointed when I tell you that your thrilling account of the Herr Doktor's heroic bargaining sessions with big, bad Bank Schwob doesn't exactly move me to tears. The same goes for the subsequent hand-wringing and soul-searching episodes. If the purblind idiot had had the elementary good sense— to say nothing of the decency—to tell me at the time about that crazy bidding for the shares, I would have told him what was happening at my end. Between us we might have made sense of all those goings-on and maybe stopped the horseplay before anyone got hurt. But no.

"Carter was in an excited state and at times barely coherent."

Wrong on two counts, Mr. L. I merely used some idiomatic English that he didn't understand. I was not in the least excited; what happened was that his stupidity finally made me hopping mad. When I phoned him that Wednesday morning, you see, I had just received another memorandum from Mr. bloody Bloch and another SESAME bulletin, and I was worried sick. If you'd been in the spot I was in you'd have been worried, too, believe me.

I have been called a lot of things in my time, but nobody has yet suggested that I am a simpleton. I will admit that in the beginning I did kid myself a little about those bulletins; I did so by trying to explain them away in terms of Bloch's own declared intentions, but that phase didn't last long. I mean if you could go on believing that the SESAME bulletins were nothing more than harmless little efforts to drum up trade with the button-pushers in the Pentagon and elsewhere, you'd have to be feeble-minded. After the CIA-scripted ham act put on by Goodman and Rich, I couldn't even pretend to believe.

So what was I to believe instead?

It's all very well for you, Mr. L. You know the score. I didn't then. And it's all very well for Val to be so wise. *By the way, she would never have talked about me in that cold-blooded, pseudo-analytical way before she started going around with that psychiatrist. Never. She's not the same any more.*

Where was I? Oh yes. What was I to think?

Well, this'll make you laugh, Mr. L, it really will.

I had begun to have a nasty suspicion that the business that Herr Bloch and his mysterious clients were engaged in was not peddling arms but peddling secrets. Isn't that a laugh? I suspected that what they were doing with *Intercom* was to use it as a shop window. Why not? Calculated indiscretion. "You want the juiciest secrets, we have them. Here's a sample of our wares to show you that the quality's right. Send for our free booklet today or call Arnold Bloch Associates direct." There are lots of smart cookies operating on the fringes of the intelligence racket. The introduction of modern sales methods in the world's second oldest profession may be overdue.

How was I to know that what they were really peddling was silence?

All right, let's not get rhetorical. Let's forget about what I thought or didn't think. This is what I did.

That night, after Goodman and Rich had left and Val had told me what she had found out about Comrade Skriabin, I decided that the first order of business next day would be to get hold of Arnold Bloch and ask him what the hell he was playing at. I decided, too, that until I had seen him, and until he had satisfied me both that my suspicions were unfounded and that there was a good reason for publishing this weird stuff he was sending me, I was going to hold back on it.

Then when I got to the office the following morning there was this second memorandum from Bloch.

TO: *Theodore Carter, Geneva*
FROM: *Arnold Bloch, Munich*
SUBJECT: *Security*

CONFIDENTIAL

Publication of the SEASAME *bulletins in recent weeks has, I am glad to tell you, had a most satisfactory effect on the markets in which my associates are primarily interested. For your private information I can state that the bulletins have been instrumental in securing important business for our French friends and in opening up avenues of approach which we had previously been obliged to consider closed. The prospects for the future appear to be excellent. Needless to say, your cooperation and strict attention to the letter of your instructions have contributed substantially to this desirable state of affairs. You may be sure that this contribution will not go unrewarded.*

As was to be expected, however, our associates' competitors have sought to counter the thrust of this novel promotion policy by attempting to discredit it. We have been reliably informed that efforts have recently been made to persuade certain western government agencies, including, it is said, the BND (Bundesnachrichtendienst), to bring pressure to bear upon us to discontinue publication of technical information, on the extraordinary grounds that by openly breaching Warsaw Pact security controls we are inviting reprisals by the Soviet authorities.

It will be immediately apparent to you that submission to such pressures would be quite inconsistent with the traditional anti-communist, anti-Soviet-bloc policies of Intercom. *Should any approaches of this kind be made to you in your capacity as editor you should reject them immediately in those terms. You should point out also that you yourself have, in any case, no discretion in the matter. You implement a policy laid down by the owners of Intercom Publishing Enterprises A.G. If pressed you should at once refer the person or persons making the approach to me. I need not remind you that any interference with a Swiss business enterprise by any foreign government agency of the kind mentioned above would not be tolerated by the Swiss security services. It may be necessary, however, to remind others of this fact should the occasion arise.*

I would appreciate prompt reports to me by telegram of any such approaches, so that steps may be taken to prevent their repetition. The agency concerned should be identified simply by its nationality (e.g., German, American, British, etc.) and the nature of the argument used discreetly stated. The circumstances of the approach and the manner in which it was made should also be briefly described.

The importance of maintaining our inde-

*pendent position and our absolute right to
publish technical and scientific information of
interest to our readers "without fear or favour" cannot be too strongly emphasised. We
must show no weakness, display no disposition
to compromise and refuse to be intimidated.
Firmly held, our position is unassailable, and
both our competitors and those dubious allies
whose aid they have solicited will soon learn
to recognise the fact.*

I enclose SESAME *Bulletin Number Six for
inclusion in next week's issue. Bulletin Number Seven, which will discuss in detail current
NATO purchasing policies, should reach you
in a few days. It may be expected to arouse
considerable international interest and contro-
versy.*

Bloch

By the time I had finished reading that I was
really confused. That memorandum threw me for a
loop. I reacted more or less as Dr. Bruchner reacted when he received the telegram from Bloch
quoting his asking price for the *Intercom* shares. I
began to wonder if Arnold Bloch and his associates
were quite sane.

I looked at Bulletin Number Six.

It was headed "Electrets Employed Successfully
in New Torpedo Guidance System."

All I was able to get from the bulletin itself was
that the Royal Naval Scientific Service (*sic*) of the
British Ministry of Defence had come up with a
torpedo, for use by antisubmarine submarines, with
a novel guidance system employing ceramic electrets in the timing and memory-storing elements.
The rest was a page of technical gibberish.

I didn't even know what an electret was. Since
the Royal Navy evidently did know, I tried looking
it up in the thirteen-volume Oxford dictionary. It
wasn't there. I found it, though, in the big Webster.

An electret is, I quote, "a dielectric body in which a permanent state of electric polarization has been set up." If that means anything to you, Mr. Latimer, congratulations.

All it meant to me was that Bloch was apparently still convinced that his associates' interests were best served by blowing military secrets and that he didn't seem to mind whose secrets he blew. The NATO boys were having the pin pulled on them just as often as the Warsaw Pact lot. As a way of making friends in high places, unless the high places you happened to be thinking of were in Red China or the Organisation of African Unity, I couldn't see it. If Arnold Bloch weren't a complete nut, he obviously had to know something I didn't.

I turned to the memorandum again and, as I re-read it, became more and more confused. I also became angry. It was that paragraph of exhortation that needled me.

I know, Mr. L, you say that that's why it was put there—to needle me into acting against my better judgment. Well, I disagree. Don't forget, I've met your "Colonel Jost," and he didn't strike me as having the kind of subtlety you claim for him. In fact, what needled me about that paragraph was the crude impertinence of it. "We must show no weakness, display no disposition to compromise and refuse to be intimidated." Pompous bastard! For me, remember, this was Arnold Bloch speaking, and that was the thing that really stuck in my throat. I may not have always been Mr. Valiant-for-Truth, but I wasn't taking lectures on the freedom of the press and the obligation to publish without fear or favour from a bloody PR man.

Rereading that memorandum didn't change my mind about a thing. It only made me more determined than ever to meet with Bloch personally, or at least talk to him. There were questions I meant to have answered. I also wanted his reaction to the news that it was the CIA and not the BND (West

German intelligence to you, Mr. L) who were after our blood, and that I, for one, was beginning to see their point.

That's when I started telephoning.

When I found that I couldn't raise Munich, I drafted a telegram.

> MEMORANDUM RECEIVED TODAY. APPROACHED YESTERDAY BY AMERICANS QUERYING SESAME SOURCES ON GROUNDS BULLETINS AGAINST U.S. INTERESTS. MANNER OF APPROACH OFFENSIVE AND TRUST MY REFUSAL REVEAL SOURCES EQUALLY SO. HOWEVER, WHILE NATURALLY RE-MAINING UNRESPONSIVE PRESSURES OF THIS OR ANY OTHER KIND MUST EXPRESS MY CONCERN SEVERAL ASPECTS OF BULLETIN CAMPAIGN IN-CLUDING PROBABLE ADVERSE EFFECT ON MA-JORITY READERSHIP AND SUBSCRIPTION RE-NEWALS. CONSIDER MEETING DISCUSS FUTURE POLICY WITH YOU THIS WEEK ESSENTIAL. PLEASE NAME TIME AND PLACE.
>
> CARTER

Polite but firm, I thought. I had made it plain (a) that his pious admonitions were not only be-lated but also unnecessary, and (b) I had served no-tice on him that, although I had so far obeyed his orders without asking too many questions, I was not prepared to go on doing so indefinitely.

When I had given Nicole the telegram to send off I felt better.

Lunch is my main meal of the day and usually I go to a brasserie near the office in the rue du Rhône. The food there is good, it is not too ex-pensive and there is no formica or chromium plat-ing visible. At lunchtime it is patronised mostly by businessmen with offices in the quarter, not the Chase Manhattan-Du Pont-Chrysler set, but middle-income managerial Genevese with growing families and houses in the south-bank suburbs. It is not a hangout for newsmen. I was surprised then when

I saw Emil Stryer come in, and even more surprised when, catching sight of me, he came across and asked if he could join me at my table.

Stryer has an Austrian passport but is said to have been born in Pomerania. He first came to Geneva to cover the 1963 Disarmament Conference for the Bulgarian Telegraphic and Radio News Agency. He had returned, after covering the Nuclear Test Ban Treaty signing in Moscow, to head the agency's small Central European bureau and had since then supplemented his income from that source by acting as a stringer for several East German, Austrian and Italian newspapers. He takes a keen interest in East-West cultural exchange programmes and has been responsible for inflicting on patient Swiss audiences a troupe of Bulgarian folk dancers, a Ruthenian puppeteer and an East German string ensemble. At the time I am speaking of he was regarded by most other members of the foreign-press corps in Geneva as something of a joke. He is a skinny little man with dark brown eyes, sallow pendulant cheeks and the perplexed, insecure look of an elderly dachshund. I did not regard him as a joke; I did, though, find him personally a very tiresome bore and generally tried to avoid him. His belief that I was an enthusiastic ideological adherent of the American imperialistic hyena Novak had helped to keep him at a distance, and I always tried to foster it.

As he sat down I said: "The General may no longer be with us, Stryer, but his soul goes marching on. Isn't it rather dangerous for you to be seen hobnobbing with me?"

He gave me an uneasy smile. "Hobnobbing?"

I paraphrased it for him in German.

He looked reproachful. "Several of our colleagues," he said, "have felt that since your proprietor's death you have been avoiding them. There has been concern for you lately, and many solicitous inquiries."

"Well, that's nice to know. As you see, I'm still managing to eat."

"The hope was expressed, and more than once, that you would return to news work of a more conventional kind."

"Less disreputable you mean? More respectable?"

"The words are yours, but, since you have employed them, why not? You have many good friends in the profession."

"But as it is, while I may not be very respectable, I am still virtually my own boss."

His eyebrows shot up. "Are you indeed? That is interesting. There has been much curiosity about your late proprietor's successor."

The waitress came up at that moment to take his order and I wondered if the interruption would break his train of thought. I didn't really expect it to do so—once started on a subject bores can never let go— but one always hopes.

He ordered *Bundnerfleisch,* a choucroute and beer and returned to the charge. "Nobody seems to know anything about him," he said.

"About who?" I wasn't going to help him out.

"I speak of Arnold Bloch, of course."

It didn't surprise me that he knew Bloch's name. Reporters gossip amongst themselves and, since Novak had died in Geneva and *Intercom,* disreputable though it might be, was published there, curiosity about his successor would be natural. Goodman's knowledge had disconcerted me because he had obtained it the hard way by going to Bâle and interviewing Dr. Bruchner. He could probably have learned as much over drinks in the Intercontinental bar.

"Oh well," I said, "there's nothing very much to know. He's a PR man."

"Public relations? Is that all?" He sounded disappointed.

"Industrial public relations. Offices in Munich, Paris and Rome."

"I see," he said and nodded thoughtfully.

I was glad he saw, because at that point, Mr. L, I was beginning to feel rather like you described Dr. Bruchner as feeling when Goodman was quizzing him—reluctant to admit that I didn't know a thing about the man I was supposed to be working for and acutely conscious of the fact that *I* hadn't even spoken to him on the telephone. Dr. Bruchner had at least done that.

I was wondering how best to field the next batch of questions when Stryer suddenly began waving frantically across the room as if he had just caught sight of a long lost friend.

I looked up. A man and a woman had entered the restaurant and now, seeing Stryer, they headed towards us.

Okay, Mr. Latimer, I know. It was a planned encounter, a put-up job. Stryer had gone to the brasserie knowing that he would find me there (he probably followed me from my office to make sure) and for the express purpose of introducing those two persons to me under circumstances which would make them appear inoffensive and harmless.

The attempt was only partially successful. Stryer made mistakes. For example, when he first came in he asked me if he might join me before he sat down. As I was alone at a table for four I couldn't very well say no. But when those two came over and joined us, he didn't even think of asking. Maybe he was nervous, too eager to get the job over and done with. Suddenly it was his table and he was the host. I remember thinking that, if it was going to be his party, he could bloody well pay for my lunch as well. However, the real snag from his point of view was the woman. Nothing he could have said or done would have made her appear inoffensive and harmless where I was concerned.

Madame Coursaux was somewhere in her forties, a junoesque welterweight with greying black hair, a muddy complexion and the smouldering eyes of a martinet. Her mirthless smile issued the challenge, her tip-tilted nose was poised to detect the answering smell of fear and her overdeveloped jaw muscles proclaimed that any attempt to defend yourself would be mercilessly punished. She wore a military-looking blue cloth coat with massive brass buttons and she walked like a grenadier. A ball-crusher if ever I saw one.

Pierre Morin, the man with her, was a burly fellow with an untidy brown beard, half-glasses and a heavy deposit of cigar ash on his waistcoat. In one large freckled hand he carried with ease a bulging pigskin briefcase which shook the floor when he dumped it beside my chair. He had bushy eyebrows, long, tobacco-stained teeth and an expression, which seemed permanent, of amused disbelief.

Both of them spoke Parisian French.

"Madame Coursaux," Stryer explained breathlessly when he had performed the introductions, "is the distinguished French expert on rare and ancient manuscripts."

She cooed at him as she removed her gloves. "You must try to get it right, Emil dear." Her eyes shifted to me. "Monsieur Carter, is it? Well, Monsieur Carter, Emil is maintaining his reputation as a journalist. Only three errors of fact in one sentence."

She ignored Stryer's whimpers of protest. She was zeroed in on me now.

"Unhappily," she went on, "I cannot claim to be an expert. The expert is Pierre Morin here. I am only a poor dealer. And the manuscripts I deal in mostly are not ancient. That is, of course, unless you call the nineteenth century ancient."

Morin joined in the game.

"While when you speak of rarity," he said, "you introduce a contradiction in terms. A book can be rare, a piece of fine porcelain can be rare. But a holograph manuscript can never be. If it is genuine it is unique, whether it was written yesterday or a hundred years ago." He grinned suddenly. "Don't let us spoil your lunch, Monsieur. Emil is used to our nonsense, eh, Emil?"

Stryer was beaming as if they had been paying him compliments. "I am always willing to be educated. But tell me—" he lowered his voice—"have you been successful in your mission? Or is it too early yet to say?"

Madame Coursaux frowned repressively and her eyes flickered in the direction of the waitress hovering behind them with menus. "We have hopes," she said curtly.

They ordered enormous meals and a Valais wine. I asked for coffee.

The moment the waitress had gone Stryer returned to the subject of the Coursaux-Morin mission.

"Carter is a journalist, as I am, but he too knows how to be discreet," he said. "May I tell him about your mission in Geneva, Madame? It is fascinating. A detective story."

His persistence seemed suicidal to me, but it earned him no more than a light cuff.

"If you tell it, dear Emil, I am sure that none of the essential facts will be correctly stated. No discretion on Monsieur Carter's part should be necessary."

He sniggered ingratiatingly. "Then correct me if I am wrong, Madame. As I understand it, you heard a few months ago and from a confidential source here in Switzerland of the existence of a hitherto unknown correspondence between the nineteenth-century anarchists Alexander Herzen and Sergei Nechaev. Such a correspondence—"

"Herzen was certainly not an anarchist," Morin broke in sharply, "and Nechaev can only vulgarly be so described. Herzen was a liberal socialist and the founder of Populism. Nechaev was many things —a terrorist, a criminal, an idealist and a mountebank—but you cannot compare him with such men as Proudhon, Bakunin and Malatesta."

"I did not mean to compare them. I only wished . . ."

He got no further. Madame Coursaux took over again. "The importance of this correspondence, if it is genuine," she said, "is the light that it purports to throw on the true authorship of the Revolutionary Action Programme of eighteen sixty-eight. That is also the year of this alleged correspondence. And I say 'alleged' advisedly. Morin has his doubts about it. I, too, am undecided. True, the correspondence between them which survives and which we know to be genuine is of a very different character, but Nechaev was a man with many faces. For you, Monsieur Carter, it is doubtless difficult to understand the historical importance of a few old letters written by men of whom you have probably never heard, but to scholars and—"

I wasn't taking any more of that; I interrupted her. "What about Herzen's memoirs?" I asked. "In eighteen sixty-eight he was working on them here in Geneva. He kept a diary too. I know he didn't think much of Nechaev. He even warned Bakunin that the man was a crook. But if this correspondence that you've found is as important as you say, I can't believe that Herzen would have made no reference to it. You've checked, of course?"

She gave me a deadly smile. "Of course," she said. But I had stopped her. It was Morin who picked up the ball.

"Herzen's memoirs were extensively edited after his death," he said, "and family feeling influenced much of that editing. There was reason at the time for deleting references to Nechaev, especially friendly or respectful references."

"Because he had seduced Herzen's daughter, you mean?"

"*Tried* to seduce her." He grinned. "Nechaev was rarely successful in his undertakings. It was amusing in a way."

And he went on to give the details. I had always

thought it a sad and rather nasty story, but he seemed to find it funny. Stryer, of course, laughed his head off. I decided that I had had enough of them and called for my bill.

As I got up to go Madame Coursaux became unexpectedly effusive.

"It is so interesting," she said, "to encounter a journalist with a feeling for history. We will be here for several more days. Perhaps we shall meet again. If so, I hope we will be able to tell you the results of our researches."

I mumbled something or other and left. As I walked back to the office I decided that for the next few days I would give the brasserie a miss.

The envelope containing Bloch's latest memorandum and bulletin had been postmarked Brussels, so I did not expect an early reply to my telegram. As there was nobody in the Munich office to answer the phone, I assumed that the telegram would remain unopened until he returned. But I was wrong. He must have had someone checking his mail every day.* The reply came the following morning and from Brussels:

> INTERCOM FOR CARTER. YOUR TELEGRAM RECEIVED AND ALL CONTENTS NOTED. REGRET MEETING THIS WEEK IMPOSSIBLE. AS POLICY UNCHANGED CONSIDER MEETING IN ANY CASE UNNECESSARY AT THIS TIME. ALSO UNNECESSARY YOU REMAIN UNRESPONSIVE TO OUTSIDE PRESSURES WISHING DISCLOSURE SOURCES. OFFENSIVE ATTITUDE YOUR PART UNDERSTANDABLE BUT INAPPROPRIATE THIS CASE. YOU ARE HEREBY AUTHORISED TO NAME ME AS SOURCE

---

*He had. The Anglo-American Stenographic Bureau, a Munich secretarial agency, had a key to his mailbox in the foyer of the office building. "Bloch" used to telephone the Bureau every weekday at 5:00 P.M., when letters and telegrams picked up earlier would be opened and read to him. This service was paid for monthly by cheque on Bloch's Munich bank.—C.L.

ALL SESAME BULLETINS UPON REQUEST AT
SAME TIME OFFERING PUBLISH CORRECTION OR
RETRACTION IF OTHER PARTY PREPARED SUP-
PLY WRITTEN EVIDENCE IN JUSTIFICATION.
YOU ARE ALSO AUTHORISED TO ADD BY-LINE MY
NAME ALL FUTURE BULLETINS IF YOU CON-
SIDER THAT COURSE ADVISABLE BUT DECISION
TO DO SO OR NOT IS SUBJECT YOUR EDITORIAL
JUDGMENT. ACKNOWLEDGE.

BLOCH

I didn't like it a bit. I had counted on my suggestion that we were losing subscribers and circulation to lure him into a meeting. Most owners would
have reacted sharply and with yelps of alarm to
that particular stimulus. He had simply ignored it.
At the same time he had deprived me of the only
good excuse I had for holding back on the bulletins
—and rather cunningly too. What he had left to my
editorial judgment was not the exclusion or inclusion of the bulletins but merely the presence or
absence of a by-line. He was exercising his authority as owner while relieving me, if I chose to be
relieved, of some share of the incurred responsibility. And why was it "inappropriate" to maintain the
traditional editorial right to protect news sources?
I tried to draft a reply which would let him know
that his evasions had been recognised as such and
make it clear that my acknowledgment of the message was not to be construed as passive agreement
with and acceptance of its contents; but I found it
impossible to be brief without sounding a good deal
snottier than is proper, or wise, for an editor addressing an owner. What I really needed, I decided
finally, was a heart-to-heart talk with the man.
Meanwhile, I would write him a letter setting out
the problems as I saw them, let him know in my
telegram of acknowledgment that a letter was on
the way and keep on trying to reach him by telephone.

In the hope that he would have returned from Brussels by then, I tried again on the Friday morning.

I, too, had a chat with the Munich police.

I didn't think much about that at the time. Offices do sometimes get broken into, usually by small-time thieves looking for typewriters, desk adding machines and petty cash. We know now that there was nothing in Bloch's Munich office worth stealing, but I'll tell you who I think it was that did the breaking and entering.

In my opinion the BfV were responsible.

Not to be confused with the BND, Mr. Latimer. The BND is the West German CIA and used to be known as the Gehlen Bureau. The BfV (*Bundesamt fur Verfassungsschutz*, or Federal Office for the Protection of the Constitution), is the West German equivalent of the FBI in its spy-catching role, the British MI5 and the French DST. That bulletin about the FG115 plane must have put them in a real tizzy, though the timing rather suggests that they were prodded into doing something about it by the CIA.

It goes like this. On Monday, December 12, Goodman and Rich interview Dr. Bruchner in Bâle and discover that Bloch is the owner of *Intercom*. They are told, however, that I do all the work and am responsible for the letter's content. So on the Tuesday they interview me. I won't talk, so they think about Bloch again.

This bit is guesswork, but I believe that on the Wednesday they went to Munich to try to see him. When they failed to do so, I would say that Rich talked things over with the Bonn CIA people, who advised consultation with the BfV. Probably the BfV had already done some checking on Bloch and found that nobody, including the Munich police and the bank, really knew a thing about him. It must have puzzled them. When the CIA started pressing for information they would feel that they had to act. I think they staged the burglary so that they could take a quick look through Bloch's private files without alerting him to the fact that he was being investigated. They wanted him back there for questioning.

Of course, they had no reason then to suspect that Arnold Bloch did not exist, that he was only a voice and a name; a voice calling long-distance from unknown places; a name posing as an identity on a set of false papers, a few bank record sheets and a series of expendable accommodation addresses.

I had no reason to suspect either. I spent most of that Friday afternoon writing to him.

It was a masterly piece of work, Mr. L. I stated the problems thoughtfully and in temperate language, went on to a cogently reasoned discussion of the solutions I proposed and wound up with a suggested agenda for a summit meeting. However, since the whole letter was predicated on the naïve assumption that the person I was addressing was a man and not a ghost and on my belief that he was more interested in our staying in business than in getting away with murder, I won't bore you with it.

I left the office just before six and stopped for a drink at the café on the corner. I had done the same thing on the two previous evenings. Since the Goodman-Rich interview I had been edgy, and, having been tailed home once before, I wanted to know if and when it happened again. Have you ever been followed, Mr. L? Probably not. If you have, though, you'll know. It gives you the willies.

From that particular café you could see along three streets. You could also enter and leave by different doors if you wanted to. I've been told that there is no simple way of evading a really determined surveillance by trained personnel, but that the subject who knows or suspects that he is being tailed can make the job difficult if he wants to. I wanted to make it as difficult as possible. As I say, being followed gives you the willies, but, unless you happen to have an unusually guilty conscience, it also makes you mad.

I don't know for certain that I was followed when I left the café to walk to my car that evening—I had spotted the Fiat with the Fribourg plates purely by accident and at a time of night when the streets in that quarter were virtually empty—but in view of what followed I am pretty sure that I must have been. I am equally sure that I gave the bastards trouble—not as much trouble as they gave me, of course, but it's nice to believe that I wasn't a complete pushover.

When I had had my drink on the glassed-in terrace, I left the money for it on the table and stood up as if I were about to leave. Then, instead of leaving, I turned and went inside past the service counter and downstairs to the telephone booths. I didn't stop there, but went on past the lavabos and up the staircase leading to the small restaurant section back of the terrace on the far side. There was a door to the street there. Outside I turned right, instead of left as I would have done if I had been going directly to my car. It was a narrow, one-way street and I was walking against the traffic towards an intersection where the lights were just changing. The moment they went to green and the cars started coming, I crossed the road quickly in front of them and cut down an alleyway that led to the river near the Pont de la Machine. Then I went into a bar and had another drink before taking to the streets again. It was just before seven when I reached my car.

It was a rear-engined Renault Dauphine—not, I admit, the most glamorous thing on wheels, but good enough for my workaday needs and Val's ski weekends, and generally reliable.

Well, I unlocked it, got in, did the usual things and found it wouldn't start. The starter was okay, the battery was okay, the meter showed that the tank was half full, but it still wouldn't start.

I'm not very good with cars, but some things about them I do know. I know, for instance, that gas-tank meters have been known to stick. I got out, raised the hood, undid the filler cap and rocked the car until I could hear the gasoline sloshing around inside. I replaced the cap.

If I had been left to my own devices, my next ineffectual move would have been to get a flashlight from the glove compartment and see if there was anything visibly wrong with the engine; but at that moment the headlights of a car turning the corner by the church dazzled me. Then, as the lights swung away and I started to go around my car, a Citroen DS skidded to a halt right beside me and a door opened.

"Trouble, Monsieur Carter?" The voice was that of Madame Coursaux.

As she spoke the rear door of the Citroen opened. Even if I had thought of running it would have been difficult to do so. I was boxed in by the two doors and the side of my own car.

Roof lights had come on in the Citroen. Morin was at the wheel with Madame Coursaux beside him. Another man sat in the back.

"We caught sight of you as we turned the corner," said Morin. "Do you need help?"

"I can't start it," I said. "I don't know what the trouble is."

"Battery?"

"No, and I've plenty of gasoline. It just won't start."

"You need a mechanic. Get in and we'll take you." The man in the back moved over to make room for me.

"That's very kind of you, but there's a garage just down the hill. It's not far. I can easily walk."

"Nonsense. Get in."

So I did. The garage was only three blocks or so

away, but when someone offers to save you even
a short walk like that, it's easier to accept than refuse. As I sat down beside the man in the back,
though, I remembered something.

"Just a moment," I said. "I've left the ignition
key."

Morin flapped a hand impatiently. "If the car
won't start nobody is going to steal it," he said.
"Besides, the mechanic will need the key."

As he spoke, the man beside me reached across
smartly and pulled the door shut. Then he put out
a meaty hand and introduced himself.

"Schneider," he said.

He pronounced it as a Frenchman would, but I
didn't think he was French. He smelled too strongly
of lavender water. I couldn't see him very well, but
the impression I got was of a heavy-bodied young
man in dark clothes with a doughy, lopsided face
and slicked-down sandy hair. He pressed my hand
briefly and without undue force.

Morin was speaking over his shoulder as he drove
off. "There is a Renault agency near our apartment.
We'll telephone them and ask them to send a mechanic."

I don't like being managed. "There's no need for
that," I said; "if you'll just drop me off at the bot-
tom of the hill that'll be fine."

He ignored me completely and at the next corner
made a left turn.

"Look . . ." I began.

"Ah no, Monsieur Carter." The woman had
turned right around to coo at me over the back of
her seat. "Leave it to Pierre to do what is best.
There is a cold wind tonight. Why stand about in
it when you could be enjoying a glass of whisky
and some friendly conversation? We met so briefly
the other day and one cannot speak of serious things
with that imbecile Stryer present."

"It's very kind of you, but I am expected home
for dinner."

"But you cannot drive to your home until your car is repaired. As soon as we have arranged for the mechanic you can telephone your daughter and explain that you have been a little delayed. It will be so much simpler."

I didn't answer. Until then I had only been irritated by what seemed to me to be high-handed behaviour on Morin's part. Suddenly things were different. When a man of my age says that he is expected home for dinner, the casual acquaintance normally assumes that he is expected by his wife, not by a daughter. These acquaintances knew too much about me to be casual. That was the moment when I began to get worried.

I glanced at Schneider. He had a sociable grin on his face. It broadened as our eyes met. He began speaking English.

"A little of what you fancy does you good," he said, "eh, Mr. Carter?"

He had a London accent, but not a very convincing one; bogus BBC out of Berlitz. I stared at him blankly.

He was still grinning. "That is what the British say, isn't it?" he persisted.

He seemed to expect a reply, so I gave him one. "I'm a Canadian, Mr. Schneider. I think that under these circumstances I'd be more inclined to say 'phooey.'"

He laughed heartily. Morin chuckled. Even Madame Coursaux managed an appreciative little snicker.

For a moment or two there we were the best of friends.

I knew the Chateau Europa, the apartment building to which they took me. There are one or two others like it in Geneva, featureless stacks of box-like service flats, all furnished exactly alike and most of them used just as *pieds-à-terre*—by tax-dodging foreigners technically domiciled in the canton who need a legal place of residence in it, by itinerant businessmen who need a staging area where they can keep the spare suit and the change of underwear, and by local pillars of society who need a place outside the home in which to entertain their girl friends. The few tenants who live permanently in such apartments keep themselves to themselves; they are interlopers in a community of absentee occupants, transients and sometime lovers. These rooms are as impersonal as, and not much larger than, the cubicles in a public lavatory—though, when you are inside one with the door shut, rather more secluded. In an apartment at the Chateau Europa there is no attendant to hear if you shout for help.

They took me to a two-roomed apartment on the fourth floor.

I say they "took" me because that's the way it was. Nobody uttered threats or held a gun on me, but their whole attitude, their decisive movements and air of confidence made it unmistakably plain that any further attempt on my part to reject their hospitality would be regarded as ill-mannered and ridiculous and firmly overridden.

As Morin pulled up in the Chateau Europa parking lot, he whipped out of the car like an attentive chauffeur and came around to open the door beside me. As I got out, Schneider slid out too. From that moment until we reached the apartment, I was between them with Madame Coursaux bringing up the rear. None of them touched me, but they kept very close. Going through the swing door Morin moved ahead and Schneider dropped back behind me. The same thing happened when we went into the elevator. It was as ordered as a drill manoeuvre. And all the way from the car to the elevator, Madame Coursaux chattered incessantly like an overanxious hostess at the beginning of a dull party.

"Hotels are such unfriendly places to stay in, don't you think? Always when I travel—and I have to travel so much in connection with my work—I try to avoid staying in hotels. A little apartment is so much better, a place where one can entertain one's friends in comfort and privacy. I know that some of my business colleagues never leave their offices. They wait for others to bring them the properties, the so-called professional finders. I will never employ such persons. Some are dishonest, most of them know so little that they are useless. I have always been my own finder and so accustomed myself to travel. But *how* one travels, ah, that is the important thing . . ."

As camouflage it was curiously effective. Nobody we encountered on the way could have suspected that I was being taken anywhere against my will. If we left any impression at all behind us it was one of three luckless men dogged by a large woman who never stopped talking.

She did stop, though, and abruptly, as soon as we were inside the elevator. Her job was done. Morin took charge from then on.

He closed the inside gate and pressed the fourth-floor button.

"But," he said, "it is our friend Carter's work that interests Monsieur Schneider here." His disbelieving smile enveloped both of us. "Did you know that he is one of your most faithful readers, Carter? But of course you didn't. How could you know?"

"And knowing, why should he care?" Schneider inquired affably. "I am one of many, many thousands."

"Eight thousand to be exact," I said.

Now that he was in a strong light I could see that he was not as young as I had thought and that his face had skin grafts and scar tissue over most of the left side. It was that that gave it the lopsided look. I had seen faces like that on ex-fighter pilots and ex-crew members of burnt-out tanks. The association made the smell of lavender water that billowed around him oddly disagreeable.

"If we were to measure a publication's influence

by the size of its circulation," Morin was saying, "we would be driven to some strange conclusions." The elevator stopped at that moment but he went on talking as he wrenched the gates open and led the way out and along the corridor. "Ask yourself. Which newspaper had the greater impact upon events, the greater historical importance, in France during the occupation? The great *Le Matin* in the hands of the collaborators, or the little *Résistance,* which the Nazis could silence in the end only by killing its editor? Ah!"

The exclamation was one of satisfaction. Madame Coursaux, acting in her new, subordinate capacity, had nipped ahead smartly as we approached apartment number 423 and already had the door open and the lights on. Morin flung off his topcoat and waved it like a cape to usher me inside.

In the cramped passageway that connected the two rooms of the apartment Schneider helped me out of my coat. Morin was already at a small built-in refrigerator extracting bottles and a bucket of ice.

"First things first," he said to me. "Whisky-soda?"

"Thank you, but I'd like to do something about getting my car fixed too."

He snapped his fingers as if in vexation at his absentmindedness.

"These *garagistes* take more notice of a woman," Madame Coursaux put in quickly. "What is the number of the car?"

I gave her the number. She repeated it once and then went into the bedroom, closing the door behind her.

"Everything under control," Schneider said, airing his English again. He motioned me to go ahead of him into the living room.

It had wall-to-wall carpeting with one of those mixed-mucus-and-mud patterns that are supposed to prevent stains showing. The furniture consisted of tubular steel armchairs—the kind without rear legs

127

that make people look as if they are sitting on air—a tile-topped table with a wrought-iron base, a unit bookcase and a blue divan with little red cushions on it. The radiator was extremely efficient and the atmosphere was stifling.

Schneider pressed me into a chair and sat himself down on the divan. Morin bustled in with a tray and began to mix drinks on the bookcase.

Except for the clinking of ice cubes in glasses there was silence for a moment. Then Schneider leaned forward with a smile.

"Monsieur Carter," he asked softly, "has anyone ever tried to kill *you?*"

I stared at him blankly. The plastic surgery on his face had evidently done something to the nerves on the left side because only the right side smiled. The effect, when he looked directly at you, was disconcerting.

"I was thinking," he went on, "of what Morin was saying just now about the editor of *Résistance* who was killed by the Nazis."

"Not only the editor, in fact," said Morin. "They murdered the whole of the staff, including the printers. Not unnaturally the paper ceased publication."

He put a large drink into my hand.

Schneider shook his head sadly. "Swine," he said.

Morin shrugged. "Oh yes, they were swine. Who can deny it? But consider." He brought over two more drinks and handed one to Schneider. "Look at it from their point of view." He lowered himself into the chair facing me. "That paper was publishing things they didn't like, things that endangered their security. What could they do? The only way to censor it was to kill those who produced it. It was natural enough in the circumstances."

Schneider nodded. "That was why I asked Monsieur Carter if there had ever been attempts on his life. After all, he publishes many things that must be objectionable to those with important interests. I would say that in some quarters he must be a highly unpopular person."

"Highly unpopular, yes," echoed Morin.

They were both looking at me expectantly now, as if they were waiting for me to reply to a toast. I took a drink and choked slightly; it was neat whisky.

"If everyone who was highly unpopular qualified for assassination," I said, "we'd have the world population problem solved in no time."

They both laughed so heartily that for a moment I thought that I must have said something funny; but, of course, they would have laughed at anything I had said just then. I'm told that they always go into the jollyboy, all-smiles routine before they get to the real arm-twisting; the idea, an erroneous one in my experience, is that it lulls the victim into a sense of false security.

In the middle of the knee-slapping Madame Coursaux came in, grinning in response to the sounds of merriment, and helped herself to a drink.

"A mechanic has gone to your car," she said as I stood up.

"I am most grateful to you, Madame." I put my drink on the table. "In that case I had better be getting back to it myself."

"Quite unnecessary, Monsieur. They will telephone to let us know when it is ready."

When I hesitated Morin reached out a freckled paw and tamped me down. "Oh, we can't let you go yet, my friend," he said. "Finish your drink, finish your drink. Then we'll see."

His grin had worn thin and there was an edge to his voice now. For a moment I considered telling him to go to hell and walking out; but, I'll be frank with you, Mr. L, I didn't have the guts to try it. You see, I was pretty certain by then that in that room I was no longer a free agent, but also too scared to put the matter to the test. I thought that it would be easier to play along with them and pretend that I wasn't scared.

With a shrug I sat back again.

"That's better." He pushed my drink across to me. "Now, Monsieur Carter, tell us all about this dangerous life you lead."

"What do you want to know?"

Morin raised his eyebrows mockingly and looked at Schneider. "He asks us what we want to know. What could be more generous than that?"

"What indeed!" Schneider got up from the divan and perched himself on the edge of the table. "I shall take him at his word. As Morin says, Monsieur, I am a faithful reader of *Intercom,* but I had not realised until a few weeks ago that you, Monsieur Carter, were a person with scientific training."

"I'm not."

"Surely you are being modest."

"Just stating a fact."

"Then you must have someone on your staff who is trained."

"No."

"So? Then how do you evaluate this scientific information you have taken to publishing recently?"

"It comes from usually reliable sources."

Morin sneered. "Ah, that precious journalistic cant! Usually reliable sources. How good it is to hear it from the actual lips of an editor. What are the others? An unofficial spokesman? A source close to the government? Yes? A presidential aide? A confidential report seen by our correspondent?"

"That last one would be a bit amateurish."

"Amateurish?" he snapped.

I had used the word because I had guessed that it would wound him and it clearly had; but I should not have tried to rub salt in.

"You'd make a poor editor, Monsieur Morin," I said. "I should have thought it was obvious. If your correspondent has seen a confidential report, naturally you don't reveal that fact. You say that he is unofficially but reliably informed, or mention an informant who does not wish to be identified. In that way you avoid compromising the person who leaked the report and at the same time cover yourself in case the leak was a calculated one."

There was a three-second silence, then Schneider pounced.

"But *you* are a good editor, eh, Monsieur?"

"Competent, I think."

"Then why do you not practice what you preach?"

"I usually do."

"You must be joking. Is it usual practice to avoid compromising an informant by publishing his name?"

"Obviously not."

"But that is what *Intercom* does, isn't it?" He leaned forward. "If I were a member of a Soviet trade mission who had spoken to you of confidential matters and then saw my name published as your informant, how would you answer my accusation of betrayal?"

I decided that the only thing to do was grasp the nettle firmly. "I take it that you are referring to a man named N. V. Skriabin," I said. "He has made no complaint to me."

"That is no answer," said Morin. "Do you know this Skriabin? Have you ever met him?"

"I know of him."

"Then if you know of him you must also know that he would under no circumstances give out the information you attributed to him."

"Why not?" I knew that I was losing my grip, so I said the only thing I could think of. "As a senior officer of the KGB he would probably have access to it."

I saw the back of Schneider's hand coming, but I had no time to protect myself. It caught me on the side of the head just above the cheekbone and almost knocked me out of the chair. For a moment I didn't quite know what was going on. Pain thudded through my head and I couldn't see clearly. Then my ears began to sing, my eyes started to water and I realised that my glasses were in my lap along with most of my drink.

Automatically I put my glasses on again and found that the frame was bent.

Schneider was looking down at me balefully. "If I were Skriabin," he said, "that would be only a beginning. Since I am not Skriabin, but only one of your readers with a special need to know the truth, you may, however, take it as a warning not to talk nonsense. Who was the person who gave you that information?"

"About the seismograph?"

"We will start with that."

I decided that the time had come for me to take Bloch at his word and let him shoulder some of the responsibility.

"It didn't come directly to me," I began. "You see . . ."

I saw Schneider's hand start to move again but Morin's moved at the same time to restrain him.

"Wait," he said. "I don't think our friend Carter yet understands the position." He turned to me. "You must believe that we are not asking these questions merely to satisfy a casual, private curiosity."

"Oddly enough," I said, "that idea had got through to me. You could have come to the point very much quicker and without all the preliminary hocus-pocus."

He ignored that. "As Schneider says," he went on earnestly, "we have a special need to know the truth. You had better accept the fact that we intend to have it."

There was a mouthful of whisky left in the glass, so I finished it off. "All right," I said, "I accept the fact. But when I'm dealing with thugs I like to know who they are. It's less boring that way. Your cover is French, so you probably aren't from SDECE. That leaves the CIA, the KGB and the BND. As a matter of interest, which are you?"

Madame Coursaux sighed gustily and came over with the whisky bottle.

"Our dossier on you, Carter, states that you are an intelligent man," she said as she refilled my glass. "If you want to get home to that excellent dinner your daughter is preparing, and in a fit state to enjoy it, now is the time to behave like one."

Morin nodded. "Sound advice, Carter. We understand your need to bolster your courage by making these childish little verbal gestures and we have been very patient so far. You now have a headache perhaps, but only a slight one. Drink some whisky, start giving responsive answers to my friend's questions and you will probably feel better."

"The other way you will certainly feel worse," said Schneider grimly. "Now, you say that the information described as coming from N. V. Skriabin did not reach you directly. Then how *did* it reach you? What was the source?"

"The owner of *Intercom,* Arnold Bloch."

"Who obtained it from whom?"

"I don't know." Schneider's face started to tighten up, so I repeated it louder. "I tell you I don't know. I received the whole story just as you read it. Not a word was altered, though I did in fact request permission to alter it."

"Why? In what way alter?"

"I wanted to omit Skriabin's name. That would be in line with our established policy of not naming sources. I wired Herr Bloch in Munich for permission to edit the name out and he replied refusing that permission."

"Did he give any reason?"

"No. I was just told to publish the story exactly as was."

"Have you proof of this?"

"I have the correspondence in the office, yes, though why the hell I should have to prove anything to you . . ."

He waved me into silence.

"You say you received it. How?"

"By mail from Copenhagen. But on Bloch's Munich paper."

"Any address in Copenhagen?"

"No. The stamps were Danish and Copenhagen was the postmark on the envelope."

"You made a statement just now to the effect that N. V. Skriabin is a senior officer in the KGB. That suggestion is not in the item you published. Did that come from Bloch also?"

"No."

"Ah, you had another source then. Who?"

"The United Nations reference library."

"No more jokes, Carter."

"I'm not joking. As I told you, I was reluctant to publish Skriabin's name. I was unhappy about doing so. I had someone check on him. Through a contact in the UN library this person dug up some biographical data on him, education, career, honours, that sort of thing. The KGB connection was deduced from the fact that his appointment to a minor trade mission was inconsistent with his earlier service record. The trade mission job was evidently a cover."

He looked at me steadily for a moment, then nodded. "We will accept that for the moment. Now, the item you published on November twentieth about Operation Triangle. What was your source for that?"

"The same. Arnold Bloch."

"But you knew what Operation Triangle was."

"No, I hadn't the faintest idea. I still haven't."

"Did you not ask?"

"It wasn't my business to ask."

"You, the editor? Not your business?"

"I was publishing technical and trade information bulletins on instructions from the owner, Herr Bloch."

"If you had been told that Operation Triangle is the code name for the first stage of an anti-ballistic missile system radar network and that it is on the NATO secret list, would you still have published that item?"

"I can't say what I would have done. That would have depended on who told me and whether or not I believed him."

"You may believe me, Carter."

"Then NATO ought to tighten up on its security procedures," I said. "I'll probably do a piece on the subject, though without quoting you, of course." He started to tighten up again, so I went on quickly. "Look, Monsieur Schneider, you're wasting your time pushing me around. Arnold Bloch is the owner of *Intercom*. He controls it. He is also an industrial public-relations consultant. Both these information bulletins you've been talking about, as well as others you haven't mentioned, were published on his instructions in order to promote the business interests of certain of his associates."

"What associates?"

"French and West German, I was told. I know nothing else about them. As for the content of these bulletins, in most cases they have been meaningless to me. I accepted them for publication from Herr Bloch on the understanding that they would be of interest to at least a section of our readership. Apparently I was not deceived. They seem to be exciting considerable interest, and you seem to know why. That's more than I do."

There was another silence, then Morin leaned forward. "Can you really be as innocent as you pretend, Carter?"

"Innocent of what?" I retorted. "Are you suggesting that something illegal has been done, that an offence in law has been committed by the publishers of *Intercom?*"

He shook his head wearily, not in denial but as if in despair at my folly. "You asked us who we were. Remember? And you asked in a particular way. Why, if you have nothing to hide and have committed no indiscretion, should you expect to be interrogated by members of foreign intelligence services?"

"Because, as Madame was kind enough to remind me, I am not a fool, and because this is not the first time this week that I have been badgered by complete strangers asking the same sort of questions."

He nodded. He did not seem surprised. A telephone had begun ringing in the next room and he waited until Madame Coursaux had gone to answer it before he went on.

"The CIA, was it?"

"Presumably, though I didn't ask them. Their methods," I added, "were less crude than yours, but they did intimate that cruder methods might be resorted to if I continued to be uncooperative. That is why I asked if you, too, were CIA. I see now that I was wrong, of course."

"Why?" demanded Schneider sharply.

"The CIA couldn't have cared less about Comrade Skriabin. They were more concerned over a story I published about a NATO fighter-reconnaissance plane."

"Did that item also come from Arnold Bloch?"

"Yes it did. Is that significant? He also supplied the story about defective Soviet rocket fuels. You could put that in your report as well."

Casually he tossed the remains of his drink into my face. A piece of ice slid down my tie to join the whisky already soaking through into my underpants.

"Now tell me about Bloch," he said. "And no more insolence."

"There's not much to tell. I've never set eyes on him. I've never even spoken to him. All our communications have been by letter or telegram. If you want to know any more you'll have to ask the man himself. In fact, he expressly instructed me by telegram today to refer inquiries about these bulletins you've mentioned—all inquiries from whatever source—to him personally. His address is . . ."

"We know his address. If we were to go with you to your office now, could we see this telegram of instruction that you say you received?"

"You could." I flicked the piece of ice from my leg to the floor. "You could also have the address of Dr. Bruchner, the Swiss director of the corporation which owns *Intercom.* He is in Bâle. After that I could show you a memorandum from Herr Bloch reminding me that any interference by foreign intelligence agents with a Swiss-based business enterprise would be viewed with serious disfavour by the federal security services. When you'd thought that over maybe we could call the police."

Schneider threw up his hands as if words had at last failed him and went to get another drink. Morin laughed. "But what would we tell the police, eh, Carter? That your car broke down? That we happened to be passing and invited you in here for a drink while your car was repaired? That while you were here conversing amicably with us you accidentally upset a glass of whisky over yourself? I don't think that the police would be very much interested in that information, do you?"

Madame Coursaux had come back into the room. "His car is ready," she said.

"Good, good." Morin chuckled waggishly. "They had no trouble, I take it, fixing the *plastique,* the bomb. Does it explode when he opens the door or when he switches on the ignition?" He raised a hand suddenly in mock alarm. "No, no. Better not say. Let it be a surprise."

I got to my feet. He stood up with me.

"Going?" he said.

"How much do I owe?" I asked Madame Coursaux.

"For what, Monsieur?"

"For having the rotor arm put back. I presume that that was what you had taken out, wasn't it?"

She stared at me blankly. Morin made a tut-tutting sound.

"My dear," he said to her, "his experiences at the hands of the CIA have given him strange ideas." He glanced at Schneider. "We must be understanding, eh?"

Schneider surveyed me coldly for a moment. Then he said: "There will be no charge, Carter, not *this* time."

He gave me a nod of dismissal. I went into the passageway followed by Morin. As he helped me on with my overcoat, he spoke softly to me.

"A word of friendly advice, Carter. There may well be a next time. We have colleagues who may have further questions to ask and suggestions to make. Don't, I beg you, compromise yourself further by going to the police or the Swiss security service. They cannot help you. You will only endanger your own interests and those of others. Remember instead what we were speaking of earlier, the fate of the men and women who worked for *Résistance*. It was not only the editor who died. You understand?"

"I understand." I just wanted to get the hell out of there.

He smiled and opened the door. *"Bon appétit,"* he said cheerfully.

I went.

My legs were very shaky, but once I got into the outside air again I felt a bit better. I started to walk back to my car.

I was three blocks away from the Chateau Europa and the headache was beginning to go when I saw the Fiat with the Fribourg plates cruise past me and park near the next intersection.

SEVEN

VALERIE CARTER
(transcribed tape interview)

My father came home looking terrible. His face was pale and blotchy, his glasses were crooked and he seemed to be having trouble breathing. He smelled strongly of whisky.

For a few moments I thought that he was drunk and had had a fall. He muttered something about having been held up and then, without taking off his overcoat, went through into the living room to look down into the street.

I went after him and got his coat off.

"What's the matter?" I asked. "Were you followed again?"

"Yes," he said, "but they seem to have gone away now. I need a drink, Val, and go easy on the water, will you?"

"Dinner's almost ready."

"I still need a drink. I may smell like a distillery, but that's mostly from outside."

I didn't argue. I had realised by then that he was upset but not drunk.

"What happened?"

He didn't tell me immediately. He said, "I've got to think, Val, I've got to think." So I gave him the drink and went back to the kitchen.

He was still standing by the window when I

brought in the tray and began to put things on the hot plate.

We had veal cutlets in a white wine sauce that evening, I remember; but I don't think either of us ate much. Over dinner he told me what had been happening to him.

I have a confession to make, Mr. Latimer. I'm not really mad about detective stories, and I don't often read them. Some of yours I *have* read, of course—those my father has in the English editions—but I only read them after I met you, because it seemed the polite thing to do and because I wanted to know how well you wrote. Of course, I enjoyed them. I think they're highly ingenious and much better written than most. Above all nobody in them is made to behave stupidly. Oh dear, all this must sound terribly impertinent and patronising, but I'm sure you know what I mean. One of the things I can't stand in that sort of book is the character who gets trapped in a dangerous situation and is forced to run appalling risks simply because he didn't, for some feebly contrived reason, go to the police when the trouble started. The author is assuming that the reader is a moron, and that's infuriating.

So, when my father began explaining why he couldn't go to the police and tell them what was going on, I became angry. Naturally that made him angry too. He became acid.

"What exactly is little Miss Great-heart proposing that I should tell the police?" he asked.

"You've said that you were kidnapped."

"Virtually kidnapped."

"And assaulted."

"What do you suggest I offer as evidence? A bent spectacle frame?"

"You could swear out a complaint."

"It would be my word against theirs—one against three."

"Yes," I said, "but they'd have to *give* their

words. They would be questioned by the police and be asked to make statements. If they are what you think they are, KGB people, they wouldn't like that. Why do you think they warned you against going to the police?"

"Because I would cause them some minor inconvenience if I did."

"Surely that's better than nothing. At least it tells them that you aren't intimidated."

"It also tells them, my dear, that my response to threats is to commit pointless and ineffectual acts of defiance. I'd rather they didn't add that to the dossier they have on me."

"Then you're just going to do nothing?"

"There's nothing to be done."

"You could at least call Dr. Bruchner and get his advice."

He didn't answer that. I don't think he really heard it. His mind was suddenly somewhere else. I went to get the coffee.

When I came back he was still staring down at his plate.

"One thing I don't understand," he said.

I refrained from saying, "Only one?" but it was an effort to do so.

"They didn't ask me what was going to happen next," he went on. "If I'd been asking the questions this evening, I'd have wanted to know whether there were any more of these bulletins in the works, and, if so, what they were about. They didn't. Morin talked vaguely about colleagues who might have further questions to ask and suggestions to make, but that was all. That looks as if their job was simply to identify the source of the bulletins and soften me up a bit for future use. He warned me not to go to the police or the federal security people, and he threatened reprisals if I did. But what he didn't say was 'Stop publishing those stories that Bloch sends you, or else.' I wonder why."

"Perhaps they're saving that ultimatum for Bloch

personally," I said. "He determines policy, not you. You told them that. Incidentally, *has* he sent you any more bulletins?"

"One, yes." He told me about the electret thing. "I suppose," he went on, "that when that goes out I'm going to have the British breathing down my neck as well."

"Then don't publish it."

"Don't be silly, Val. Of course I'm going to publish it." He got up. "Right now, though, I'm going back to the office."

"At this time of night? Why?"

He finished his wine and then poured quite a lot of brandy into his coffee. "Because," he said, "it has just occurred to me that the only evidence I have that I've been telling the truth about all this is in a file sitting in a tray on Nicole's desk—the bulletins, the correspondence with Bloch, everything. I put it there myself when I left. But after what's happened this evening, I think I'd sleep better over the weekend if that file was in a safe place."

"Would you like me to drive you?"

He shook his head. "I'll be back by the time you've done the dishes."

He finished the coffee and brandy before he left.

That was just before ten o'clock. At eleven I started to get ready for bed. The fact that he hadn't come back by then didn't worry me. Once in the office, he wouldn't pay much attention to the time, I knew. He might start working or thinking about working and forget it. By eleven-thirty, though, I was getting tired, so I decided to telephone the office and tell him that I wouldn't wait up. There was no reply. I assumed then that he had gone to a café for more brandy. There was nothing I could do about that. I went to bed.

It was at seven the following morning that the call came from the hospital.

FROM THEODORE CARTER
(transcribed dictation tape)

To tell the truth, I hadn't been completely frank with Val. When I went back to the office it wasn't *only* in order to put the Bloch file in a safe place; I also wanted to have another look at the electret bulletin before I made up my mind whether or not to publish it.

In spite of my bold words to her on that subject, the idea of inviting the British to join the rapidly growing Let's-Bug-Carter Club didn't seem to me a particularly appealing one at that moment. Not that I thought that the British would send bully-boys to slap me around and throw drinks in my face, but their intelligence people are not always as gentlemanly as they like to pretend. They can be vindictive. If they wanted to be nasty and went about it in the right way, they could probably get the Canadian embassy in Bern to rap me over the knuckles.

On the other hand, I wasn't about to throw in the towel just because things were getting a bit rough. I don't like being pressured; it makes me bloodyminded; and, while I didn't know Bloch, the fact remained that he was paying my salary. So if he wanted his goddam technical bulletins to appear in the publication he owned, who was I to say him nay? As the editor I was entitled to object on policy grounds and, if my objection were over-ruled *and* if I felt strongly enough about that, to resign. I could also object, on legal grounds, if the material sent in for publication was in my opinion libelous or obscene. While I hadn't cared for the reference to Skriabin, nobody, excepting possibly Mr. Schneider of the KGB, had suggested that it was libelous; Goodman hadn't complained that we had libelled the FG115; and, unless Webster's Third New International Dictionary had got its wires

143

crossed, there was nothing obscene about electrets. *Intercom* wasn't in business to win popularity contests. So, until someone with the authority to do so clapped a cease-and-desist order on us, it seemed to me that I had no justification for failing to carry out my owner's instructions.

I was worried all the same. By the time I arrived at the office I had made up my mind about one thing: if, after rereading the electret bulletin, I decided to go ahead and publish it, I would also exercise my "editorial judgment" and put Bloch's by-line on the story. Then, maybe, if the British felt like pushing anyone around, they would pick on him rather than me.

At that time of night I had no trouble parking near the building. I had seen nothing more of the car with the Fribourg plates.

Our offices were on the second floor. The mailboxes for the building were in the foyer. More from habit than because I expected to find anything in it, I glanced through the small glass window in the door of our box as I pressed the *minuterie* switch for the staircase lights. There was a telegram there.

I unlocked the box and opened the telegram. It was the one from Dr. Bruchner giving me Bloch's *poste restante* address in Brussels. Aside from assuring me that Dr. Bruchner still cared, it didn't seem of very much use just then. I shoved it into my overcoat pocket and went on up the stairs.

Stopping to open and read the telegram had delayed me for half a minute or so, and the lights went out while I was still on the stairs. I swore and groped my way up to the *minuterie* switch on the second-floor landing. The stairs were uncarpeted and I dare say I made quite a bit of noise before I had the light on again and my key in the lock of the office door—more than enough noise to warn anyone inside of my approach.

The lock was a pin-tumbler type with a mortice tongue; you had to use the key when you left for the night or anyone could open the door just by turning the knob. I had been the last one to leave and I was sure that I had locked up as usual. Now I found that my key wouldn't turn and that the door was unlocked.

My first thought was that the concierge had been in for some reason—he had a master key—and had forgotten to relock when he left. I pushed the door open, went in and felt for the light switch on the left.

The staircase light had gone out again by then and I was still fumbling for the inside switch when I smelled that something was wrong. Most offices have their characteristic smells. Ours was a mixture of mimeograph ink, light machine oil, stationery, the fluid used to paint out mistakes on stencils and Nicole's French cigarettes.

What I smelled now was lavender water.

My heart jolted unpleasantly and I turned to get out. At that moment a flashlight came on about two arm's-lengths away from me.

It was a powerful light and I put up my hands to shield my eyes. I think I started to say, "What the hell is this?" but I didn't finish it. As I opened my mouth there was a phutting noise like that of a beer can being opened and something puffed in my face.

A second later, with the next breath I took, the pain hit.

The stuff wasn't tear gas. I know what that's like; I had a dose of it once when I was covering a street riot in Paris. This was ten times worse—some kind of chemical Mace or nerve gas, I would say. It didn't have any distinctive smell but it acted almost instantly. First there was a tearing pain in the sinuses, then in the throat, then the chest. That was quickly followed by a feeling that the stomach was coming up fast to get out before something worse happened. It was like an explosion inside. I don't believe I lost consciousness, but the next thing

I remembered clearly was blundering about with my eyes shut, retching and fighting for breath at the same time, and then falling over a chair. I didn't try to get up. All I wanted was for the pain to stop and to be able to breathe.

I don't know how long I lay there before the stomach cramps began to go—twenty minutes perhaps—and then I was afraid to move my body in case the cramps started again. I was still in the small outer office. There were no windows there, so I was in complete darkness. After a bit I tried feeling about to see if I could orient myself. I touched the leg of the chair I had fallen over and that gave me some idea of where I was; there was only one chair in the outer office. I waited another minute or two and then crawled in the direction of the landing door. Only when I had found the door frame did I attempt to stand up. The sinuses still felt as if they had been flushed out with molten lead, but the stomach seemed to have quietened down. I found the light switch and pressed it. When I had got used to being upright again and felt that my legs were equal to walking, I skirted the mess on the floor and went to my office.

My desk had been searched, of course; the contents of the drawers were neatly stacked on top of it. The fact that the safe was open was no surprise. It had been the General's idea to have a document safe, but I had never used it for anything but account books, and, since it was of an inexpensive type designed to protect the contents against fire rather than burglars, I usually left the key in the lock.

I went through into Nicole's office. Nothing there appeared to have been disturbed. I found the Bloch file in the tray on her desk where I had left it.

A quick check told me that everything was still there. I took the electret bulletin out, put it in Nicole's typewriter and added a by-line to the caption—*From our Munich correspondent, Arnold*

Bloch. Then I ran it through the copying machine and placed the duplicate in the folder marked PRESS which held the rest of the draft copy for the next week's issue. She would start retyping it all first thing Monday morning so that I could get on with the final editing. I wouldn't have to think about it again until then.

The original of the bulletin I returned to the file. I took that back to my room. I considered locking it away in the safe and then decided that I would prefer to keep it with me. I put it in an old brief-case I had there.

My next move was to get the bottle of whisky I kept hidden behind *Who's Who in America* and the shot glass masked by *Satow's Guide to Diplomatic Practice* and try to remove the metallic taste of the gas from my mouth.

Oh yes, I thought of calling the police. I thought very carefully about it. But what could I have told them that they would have believed? That my office had been broken into? There was no evidence of a forced entry; I had looked that outer door over very carefully. That a thief had been there? But nothing had been stolen. That someone had squirted something in my face which had made me throw up? Well yes, there was evidence that I had thrown up; no doubt something I had eaten had disagreed with me. Gas? Maybe you'll be feeling better in the morning, Monsieur. I'd have been lucky if they were that polite.

I cleaned up the mess in the outer office as best I could and got rid of it in the lavabo. Then I had some more whisky. By then, I must tell you, I was feeling lousy—cold and very weak at the knees. Delayed shock probably. I definitely wasn't drunk. All I wanted at that moment was to go straight to bed.

And with any luck I'd have gone straight to bed. I put what remained of the whisky away, picked up the briefcase and switched off all the lights. Then

I opened the outer door and switched on the *minuterie*. The ritual of locking up seemed pointless— it was obvious now that anyone who had a mind to do so could open up the place with a paper clip —but I went through with it as usual. To be truthful I was glad of the excuse it gave me to delay my departure another few seconds. You see, I was scared of going out into the street; I was afraid that Schneider might be waiting for me there with reinforcements. But I had made up my mind to take *that* risk. It wasn't until I had started down the stairs and saw that CIA bastard Rich with another man I didn't know coming up towards me that I panicked.

All right, Mr. L, I know. You think that I behaved like a clown; you think that I should have stood my ground and told them politely but firmly that I only saw people by appointment during normal office hours. Well, if you think that's how *you* would have behaved if you'd been in my shoes, lots of luck. If you really mean to stir up the mud you may need it. What you have to remember is, Mr. L, that that day had been a pretty traumatic one for me. In the space of a few hours I had been snatched, interrogated under duress, roughed up, threatened, burgled and gassed. After that sort of treatment your thinking tends to become a little overpragmatic, and when you see anything that looks as if it means more trouble, you don't wait for second thoughts; you run.

So I ran.

I ran down the stairs straight at them, swinging the briefcase at Rich's face as I did so. He jerked back to avoid it and cannoned into the man behind him. I don't know whether or not they tried to grab me as I went by them. Probably not; they were completely off balance and I didn't give them time to recover. I had hold of the curved handrail by then and I went down the rest of the stairs three at a time.

Rich called something after me—something about only wanting to talk—but I didn't even think of stopping. In the Chateau Europa, Schneider had only wanted to talk. As I reached the door to the street I heard them clattering down the stairs after me.

The Fiat with the Fribourg plates was right outside and I saw the driver's face turn towards me as I ran by. My car was up the street on the other side in a zone parking place. As I reached it and opened the door I looked back and saw Rich and the other man come out and start running across the street towards me. Rich shouted my name.

Although I was gasping for breath and shaking badly I managed to fumble the key into the ignition and start up before they got to me. I drove off like a maniac.

It had been raining earlier and the streets were still wet. Turning onto the Pont de la Coulouvrenière, I skidded badly but managed to pull out of it. They closed up on me though and were about a hundred meters behind as we went up the Boulevard Fazy. I thought that I would try to lose them in the streets behind the Cornavin Station. Don't ask me why. I realise now that, even if I had lost them in the way I had hoped, all they would have had to do was drive to my apartment and wait for me to show up there. At the time I just felt that I had to get away. I decided that a sudden left turn out of the Place de Montbrillant and across some oncoming traffic might do the trick.

It did. The trouble was that I picked a narrow street with a parked truck in it to turn into and I made the turn too suddenly and too fast. I entered the street with all four wheels sliding and at an angle of forty-five degrees. With a rear-engined car you don't pull out of a skid by lifting your foot; you put on power to bring the back around and straighten up. If that truck hadn't been parked there I might have made it. As it was I had no room to manoeuvre. I put my foot down and steered into the skid, but the rear end didn't come around fast enough. I sideswiped the truck. Then, I'm told, the car mounted the kerb and hit a stone bollard outside the entrance to a porte-cochère. My head went through the windshield on impact, and I went out like a light.

That was how I got in touch with the police.

EIGHT

COMMISSAIRE PAUL-EMIL VAUBAN
Police Judiciare, Geneva
(edited tape interview*)

    The accident to which you refer occurred at
approximately 23.25 hours on Friday, December
16. The Cornavin quarter is within my jurisdiction.

    Reports of traffic accidents and other incidents
of concern to the police are normally made to the
duty officer at the commissariat. A summary of the
reports received by the night duty officer is brought
to me here in my office on my arrival in the morning. In the case of a serious crime or the suspicion
of one, I am, of course, notified by telephone at
my home no matter what the hour; but for an
apparently minor incident such as this I would not
be disturbed.

    However, when I saw the name Theodore Carter
on the morning summary report of December 17, I
at once called for further details of the case. I had,
as you evidently know, had a previous encounter
with this man, and it seemed to me that an early
exchange of information between the judiciary
branch and the Bureau for the Control of Foreign
residents might be advisable.

    The most serious charges against him at that
juncture were those of driving while drunk and

---

*Translated by C.L.

151

dangerous driving. There were, reportedly, three witnesses to the accident, one of whom was nearly hit when the car left the road. A patrol car was at the railway station nearby at the time and arrived on the scene a minute and a half later.

The *agent* in charge called an ambulance from the *polyclinique* to attend to the driver, Carter, whom he described as smelling strongly of vomit and alcohol. Blood and urine tests taken shortly after Carter's admission to the hospital showed alcohol concentrations of 320 milligrams per 100 millilitres in the blood and 440 milligrams in the urine. He had without doubt been drinking heavily. His injuries, which consisted of bruises and multiple facial cuts caused by small fragments of the safety glass, appeared to be superficial. However, he had suffered a period of unconsciousness, and, in view of this, the hospital authorities thought it advisable to detain him there until they could be certain that the concussion would have no aftereffects.

On regaining consciousness he had made a number of seemingly irrational statements about the cause of the accident. At first these were attributed to his state of intoxication. When he persisted in them later and then had to be forcibly restrained from leaving the hospital, the possibility of his having suffered serious brain damage was considered. The doctor in charge of the case decided to call in a specialist from the hospital's neuropsychiatric department for consultation.

In the light of my own experience with Monsieur Carter this seemed to me at the time an appropriate decision. I asked that I be kept informed of developments in the case.

By this time Carter's daughter had been informed of the accident and that her father was in the hospital. She did not see him immediately on her arrival there, however, because by then he was asleep.

Later that morning Mlle Carter called on me at my office.

She is, as you are no doubt aware, an extremely personable young woman. It was with profound regret that I found myself unable to comply with her request that her father should be brought before a court that afternoon and released *sous caution*. She herself, she said, was prepared to furnish the bond.

I reminded her that the charges against her father were serious, that the court would not be in session until Monday morning and that, in any case, her father was now in the care of the hospital. I told her that decisions about further police action would have to await the psychiatrist's report.

At that she became indignant. It was not an easy interview. The young today have no respect for authority. I tried as best I could to explain the difficulties of my position. In doing so I mentioned, a little caustically perhaps, the fact that her father had attempted to excuse his violations of the traffic laws the night before by pleading that he was being hounded and pursued by agents of foreign intelligence services at the time.

"And how do you know he wasn't?" she demanded brusquely.

As I did not consider that the question required a reply, I merely shrugged.

That seemed to enrage her. "Exactly. You don't know. And now—" she pointed a finger at me— "now he is also being hounded by you the police. I am ashamed."

"Mademoiselle . . ." I began, but she was not prepared to listen to reason.

"Yes, ashamed," she went on, "ashamed that I was fool enough to suggest that he should go to you for help."

She then declared that she intended to consult a lawyer and left.

In retrospect I can only say that I acted throughout with strict propriety and in complete conformity with established police practices. The case was exceptional, as you know. With insufficient information at my disposal I could only conclude at that point that both Carter and his daughter were a little mad. I consider that the criticisms of my person and conduct subsequently voiced by Mlle Carter have been unfair to the point of scurrility and totally undeserved.

Attractive though she may be, Mlle Carter undoubtedly has in her something of her father's character.

DR. MICHEL LORIOL
(written statement*)

On the morning of December 17 I was requested, in the absence of Dr. Thomas, who heads our neuropsychiatric unit, to examine a patient admitted through the *polyclinique* during the night. He had been involved in a traffic accident.

The patient was Theodore Carter.

I had a preliminary consultation with the house surgeon in charge and was given the case history, such as it was. The concussion had resulted from what appeared to have been a *contre coup* injury. X rays had established that there was no fracture. Blood pressure and pulse were satisfactory. Treatment had been confined to bed rest and intravenous injections of vitamin B_6 to hasten the metabolism of the alcohol in the patient's blood. He had slept for six hours and was now disintoxicated. Yet he was still, according to the house surgeon, talking in the same irrational way as that in which he had talked when he had been admitted to the hospital. His behaviour was aggressive. He had twice attempted to leave the hospital and had had to be restrained. As he was technically under police arrest he had been moved from the emergency ward

---

*Translated by C.L.

154

to a room in the annex. He had also been denied access to his clothes.

I went to see him.

He was sitting up in bed—a pale, grey-haired man with cadaverous, unshaven cheeks and angry eyes. He had a bruise on the left cheekbone and four of the cuts on his face had dressings over them. He peered at me myopically when I entered.

"Ah. The young Dr. Kildare, I presume," he said in English. His tone was distinctly hostile.

I introduced myself and asked if he would prefer that we conducted our conversation in English.

He replied in French that if I were prepared to talk sense he did not care which language was used; otherwise he would prefer not to talk at all It was not a good beginning.

I said I hoped that we could both talk sensibly.

"Are you a psychiatrist?" he asked.

"I am a member of the hospital neuropsychiatric unit, yes." I began to examine him.

"I think I should tell you," he said, "that I share André Gide's view of psychiatry."

"Which view is that?"

"He said that 'know thyself' was a maxim as pernicious as it was ugly, because the person who studies himself arrests his own development."

I smiled. "I know the passage you mean. He then went on to declare that a caterpillar that sets out to know itself would never become a butterfly. Quite untrue, wouldn't you say? A caterpillar can't help but become a butterfly. The process has nothing to do with knowing."

"He was speaking figuratively of course," he said crossly. "Anyway, all I was trying to establish with you was that I am neither irrational nor deranged. The padded cell and the strait jacket will not be needed."

"I am relieved to hear that, Monsieur," I replied. "Neither is available in this hospital."

After that he allowed me to complete my examination in silence. I discovered no residual signs of organic damage.

He peered at me a trifle anxiously as I straightened up. "Well, Doctor?"

"How bad is your headache?"

"Not too bad now. I've felt worse."

"Did you lose your glasses in the accident?"

"I suppose so. They probably got smashed up when I did. I tried to send a message to my daughter asking her to bring me a spare pair. They're an old prescription, but they'd be better than nothing. However, I doubt if the message was passed on," he added sourly. "That half-wit colleague of yours probably assumed that 'glasses' was a code word and that what I was really asking her to do was smuggle in a hacksaw."

"She was here earlier, but you were asleep. I understand that she'll be coming back. Would you like to tell me about the accident?"

He gave me a shrewd look. "You mean what led up to the accident, don't you? That's the story that's causing all the fuss, isn't it? That's why *you're* here." He shook his head ruefully. "I should have kept my mouth shut."

"Let's start with the accident itself," I said. "Do you remember it?"

He frowned. "Well no, I don't. Not clearly. I remember making a sharp left turn, skidding and hitting a truck. After that . . . I'm not sure. Is that bad?"

"Some loss of memory for events occurring immediately prior to a concussion is quite normal. Nothing to worry about. But you'll have to stay in bed for a couple of days. With a concussion, even a mild one, it is never safe to take chances."

"Monday is press day," he said. "Can I be out of here by Monday?"

"Possibly, but . . ."

"Oh yes, of course. I'm under arrest, aren't I?"

"Had you had much to drink?"

"I'd had quite a bit, I suppose, one way and another," he said reluctantly; "but I'd thrown up most of it."

"When was that?"

"After I was gassed," he said. He was looking at me defiantly now.

I nodded. "Tell me about the gas."

"I went back to my office to get a file I'd left there. There was someone in the office who shouldn't have been there. I have reason to believe that it was someone I knew, a man named Schneider. Anyway, he shone a light in my face and then squirted some sort of gas at me. It practically knocked me out and made me throw up."

"You say you have reason to believe that it was someone you knew. Aren't you sure?"

"It was dark. I didn't see him. But I smelled him. He uses lavender water."

"Did the gas smell of lavender water?"

He drew in his breath and then exhaled impatiently. "Doctor, why don't we just forget the whole thing?" he said. "Just tell them I'm hallucinating a bit because of the concussion and that I'll be okay in a couple of days. Right?"

"I couldn't very well tell them that," I answered reasonably. "You see I don't know that you are hallucinating, as you put it, do I?"

"Well, you're not believing a word I'm telling you, are you?"

"What I believe isn't important. It's what you believe that I'm interested in." I went on before he had a chance to reply. "Do you smoke, Monsieur?"

"Yes, I smoke, but they took away all my things. I haven't got any cigarettes here. Why?"

I offered him a cigarette and he took one, but he gave me an amused look as he did so. "Oral gratification?" he remarked with a lift of his eyebrows. "A breast symbol to reassure? Is that the idea, Doctor?"

Patients with a smattering of knowledge can be

trying. I had not intended to smoke myself, but his interpretation forced me to change my mind. I couldn't let him feel that he had taken charge of the interview. Fortunately, I still had the cigarettes in my hand. I smiled as I reached for my lighter.

"Do you think you need reassurance?" I asked.

"What I need," he replied promptly, "is a drink. But I suppose that kind of oral reassurance is out. I'll settle for the cigarette."

I lit both our cigarettes and said: "Let us go back to this man Schneider. You say that you knew him and that he smelled of lavender water."

He made a gesture of irritation. "Forget the lavender water for the moment. If I've got to tell you the whole story I'll have to go back to the beginning."

"Very well."

"I edit a newsletter called *Intercom,* Doctor. Have you heard of it?"

"I have seen a copy." I did not mention that it had been shown to me by a colleague as a classic example of transatlantic paranoia; but the guarded tone of my reply did not escape the patient.

He grinned. "I won't ask you what you thought of it, Doctor. I can guess. Well, a month or two ago *Intercom* changed hands."

His story took over an hour to tell. Once or twice, in the earlier stages, I stopped him to ask for clarification of something he had said; I wanted to see what effect interruption would have on his train of thought; but after that I let him go on without interruption. If the patient is willing to talk freely it is as well to let him do so. There was a manic quality about his way of telling it, of course, but after a while I began to suspect that this was to some extent a cultivated mannerism, part of his journalistic stock in trade. I made no attempt at that time to make a judgment about the truth of the story. If it was fantasy, it was singularly well-organised fantasy. On the other hand, it came from a man who, on his own admission, had made fantasy his business and was inclined to be proud of his success with it—a schizoid personality. I would need more evidence before I could formulate an opinion.

When he came to the end I asked two questions.

"Have you told anyone else about this? I don't mean here at the hospital, but before the accident."

"Val knows some of it."

"Val?"

"My daughter Valerie."

He had slumped down in the bed and was looking very tired. I decided to postpone further questioning.

"I'll look in and see you again later," I told him.

"You do that," he said and closed his eyes; but as I reached the door he spoke again.

"The briefcase, Doctor. I had it with me in the car. I'd like to know it's safe. And I'd like you to see the file that's in it. I think the police have what remains of the car."

"I'll see what I can do," I said.

I found the house surgeon having coffee in the staff common room. He is one of those men who expresses his distrust and ignorance of psychiatry by being facetious about it. He greeted me with an expectant grin.

"Well, what's the expert verdict?" he inquired. "Deranged or merely cracked?"

"Possibly neither."

He looked at me as if he thought that *I* was cracked.

"I'd like to speak to the daughter," I went on. "Do you know if she returned?"

"She did. But even if she's still here you won't get very much out of her. Very nasty temper she has. Says papa's been framed by the police and that we're aiding and abetting." His smile became sardonic. "I gather she doesn't think much of your specialty. Better be careful or she'll have your head off."

Mlle Carter had evidently made an impression on him. I looked forward to meeting her.

I found her eventually in an otherwise empty waiting room in the main building.

There is something I should explain here. Valerie Carter and I have come to know each other well during these past few months and I hope that we will shortly be married. I mention this because any account I give now of our first meeting is bound to be coloured to some extent by our present relationship. I can only try to be objective.

A nurse introduced me to her.

I saw an extremely beautiful young woman with a pale, clear complexion, dark, almost black hair and her father's angry eyes. She was wearing a red and black cloth coat. Her response to the introduction was disconcerting.

She gave me a nod and then said crisply, "I was told that my father was being examined by a psychiatrist. I would like to see that gentleman."

I bowed. "That is why I am here, Mademoiselle."

She stared. "You are the psychiatrist?"

"Dr. Thomas is the senior physician in charge of the neuropsychiatric unit," I said. "However, he is at present attending a professional convention in Paris. I am his assistant and I examined your father. Please sit down, Mademoiselle."

I look younger than I am. I know she wanted to ask me if I were really qualified to conduct a psychiatric examination; but she restrained herself. She would hear what I had to say first. If she did not like what she heard, *then* she would question my competence. She sat down.

"How is my father, Doctor?"

"His physical condition seems good, but with head injuries one always has to be careful. We will know better by Monday."

"You say his physical condition seems good. Do you mean that his mental condition *doesn't* seem good?" She had coloured slightly and her eyes had narrowed. I was on dangerous ground.

"That is what I want to discuss with you."

She considered me for a moment, then gave a curt nod. "Very well. But I may as well tell you, Dr. Loriol, that I have already been to see that imbecile Commissaire. He seemed to feel that the statement my father made after the accident should be treated as a joke. If that is your approach, too, any discussion between us would be a waste of time."

"My approach, Mademoiselle, is purely medical. I don't know exactly what your father said after the accident. I wasn't there. I do know that he had been drinking quite a lot before the accident. It may well be that after it he wasn't very coherent."

"My father is *always* coherent."

"He had suffered a concussion, you must remember, and been found unconscious. A period of confusion would be understandable. However, his earlier statements need not concern us now. What I am concerned with is the statement he has just made to me."

"Well?" She was still very much on her guard.

"In my opinion it calls for investigation."

"By the police, do you mean?"

"By you and me initially, Mademoiselle, if you agree. Your father told me about a series of incidents, of certain strange things that he says have been happening to him."

"Didn't you believe him?"

"I believe that *he* believes that these things happened and that they are interrelated, but that is not the point. I asked him if he had told anyone else about these strange happenings—before the accident, I mean—and he said that he has told you about some of them. Has he?"

"Of course." She looked at me a trifle pityingly.

"But how does that help you? If my father believes what he is saying, the fact that he tells me what he tells you isn't evidence that what he is saying is based on reality."

"No, but I think that you yourself were actually involved in one incident. You were there when two Americans came to his apartment and questioned him, I understand."

For the first time the suspicious, defensive look left her. "Yes, that's right. I was there."

"Your father says that they were CIA men."

"He said that one of them was. *They* said they were from a news magazine, but they certainly behaved very strangely. It was quite unpleasant."

"Would you tell me about it?"

She told me. She also told me about the inquiries she had made concerning the man Skriabin and what she had learned from her friend in the UN library. That was something that her father had omitted from his account. But it fitted in. That was the moment when I began to accept the fact that the story her father had told me, fantastic though it might be, could possibly be true.

I did not immediately say so, however, and that was a pity, in more ways than one. But I was in a difficult position. I had legal as well as medical responsibilities in the case, and extreme caution was indicated. If I concluded that the patient's account of his experiences represented fact and not fantasy, it would be necessary to defend my findings to the police and probably other law-enforcement agencies as well—for obvious reasons, I already had the federal security service in mind. The police are notoriously resistant to psychiatric evidence when it threatens to contradict their own preconceived findings. I had no reason to believe that the security service would be any easier to deal with. Before I committed myself to an opinion I would have to be certain that I stood on absolutely solid ground. I had Dr. Thomas's reputation and that of the unit to consider as well as my own.

Valerie was watching me with narrowed eyes, waiting for my reaction to what she had told me. I responded as noncommittally as I could.

"Thank you, Mademoiselle. You have been very helpful."

"I also saw the car that was following him," she said, "the car with the Fribourg plates."

"Did you actually see it following him?"

"Well no, but it was there in the street outside our apartment."

"You saw a car with Fribourg plates," I said carefully. "That isn't a very rare sight in Geneva, is it?"

She sighed. "No. I understand. It isn't evidence."

I stood up. "I expect you would like to see your father now. He said that he sent a message asking you to bring him his spare glasses. Did you get the message?"

"Yes, and I have the glasses." She too was standing now. She turned to face me. "Dr. Loriol, you can't really believe that my father is insane, can you?"

The question was both a statement of her own conviction and an appeal to me to share it with her. I regret to say that I replied evasively.

"I would be most reluctant to believe it, Mademoiselle, I assure you. His room is in the annex. If you will come with me I will show you the way."

She said no more, but I knew that I had disappointed her. In the annex I handed her over to the nursing sister in charge and then went back to my office.

There I telephoned the police and asked to speak to Commissaire Vauban. He was not available, so I spoke to a duty officer instead. I did not discuss the patient; what I wanted to know about was the briefcase with the Bloch file in it which Carter had said was in his car. The duty officer was helpful but there was not much he could do. The damaged car had been towed to the police garage. It was still there. Nothing had been removed from it and nothing could be removed from it without proper authorisation. The duty officer promised that he would mention the matter to Commissaire Vauban as soon as he could.

Almost twenty-four hours elapsed before I was allowed to examine the contents of that briefcase.

By then the damage had been done.

VALERIE CARTER
(transcribed tape interview)

At first the day had been frightening. As it wore on it became maddening.

It was at the hospital, where I went after the telephone call from the police, that I learned that my father was going to be charged with drunken driving. Then I saw that cretinous policeman Vauban. From the commissariat I went to Maître Perriot's office. He was the *notaire* my father used when he leased the apartment and made his will.

In my confusion I had forgotten that it was Saturday. Of course, Perriot's office was closed. I found his home number, however, and telephoned him. He was quite helpful until I told him about the drunken-driving charge. Then he tried to back out. I wouldn't let him; but all I could make him promise was that he would see my father on Monday at the hospital. He insisted that there was nothing he could do before. He may have been right, but I didn't think so at the time.

I had a sandwich in a café and went back to the hospital. I still wasn't allowed to see my father; instead I saw a pompous fool of a house surgeon who told me about the psychiatric nonsense and gave me the message about the spare glasses. I went and got them from the apartment. When I returned to the hospital for the third time they told me to wait.

I wasn't disappointed in Michel, in Dr. Loriol. I was furious with him. Quite unreasonably, I admit. He was absolutely right to be careful about what he said at that point, especially to me. What made me furious was his being so obviously careful. No, that's unfair. I was furious because I had tried hard to make him commit himself and failed. I wasn't in a very reasonable state of mind that afternoon.

If I had been I wouldn't have helped my father to do what he did.

When I went in he began by being shame-faced and apologetic, but that phase didn't last long—about two minutes, I would say. Then he told me what had happened the previous night when he had gone back to his office.

I was horrified, naturally, and as angry as he was. We had plenty to make us angry. I told him about Maître Perriot's weak-kneed reluctance to become involved and about my ridiculous interview with Commissaire Vauban.

He remembered the Commissaire.

"That fish-eyed phony," he said. "I might have known." He said some other uncomplimentary things about the Commissaire that I won't repeat.

I suppose we both got very worked up, or depressed and desperate, or all three, if that's possible. You see, everything looked so black that day. Here were these bogeymen, as my father called them, behaving like gangsters, and all the police did when he told them what was going on was to say that he must be insane and charge him with drunken driving. Things were in such a hopeless mess and there seemed to be no one we could turn to. I didn't even consider Michel; at that stage I thought of him as one of the enemy. It's easy to say now that, if we had been patient and wise and waited for the air to clear and truth to prevail, everything would

165

have been all right. It is as easy—and about as sensible—as telling a person who has just fallen from the top of a high building that, if he had had the presence of mind to relax all his muscles before he hit the ground, he wouldn't have broken so many bones.

I'm not trying to make excuses. I'm just explaining why it was that, when what looked like a straw came floating by, we both clutched at it.

My father had been wondering aloud if it would do any good to inform Dr. Bruchner of the situation, or whether his reaction to it would be the same as Maître Perriot's.

"He might know someone in the Federal Assembly," I said, "or even the Council."

My father shook his head. "That wouldn't do any good. The police here wouldn't take any notice of anyone in Bern. What we have to do is go over this fool Vauban's head to someone who'll listen." He paused, then added: "Or someone who can be made to listen."

"How can you *make* someone listen?" I asked wearily.

"By raising hell," he said and suddenly snapped his fingers. "Yes, that's it. Break the story. Set the dogs on them. Put them on the spot. Make 'em sweat."

I had to listen to more fighting words and finger-snappings before he could be persuaded to tell me what he meant, but when he did explain I became almost as enthusiastic as he was.

This was the plan. He would use *Intercom* to break the story of his persecution and harassment, but give the news agencies advance notice of it. In that way both the story, which he would make as sensational as possible, and *Intercom* itself would receive the maximum publicity. Commissaire Vauban's superiors would be forced to take notice. Questions would be asked. The authorities would be placed on the defensive.

My part in the operation was that of go-between. First, I had to get him writing materials, and then, when he had written the piece, take it out of the hospital. When I had made typed copies I was to deliver one to Nicole Deladoey with instructions to make it the lead story in the Tuesday issue. This was to guard against the possibility of his being prevented by the police or the hospital from going to the office on Monday. Next, I was to make French and German translations. Finally, I was to telephone a list of those foreign news-agency correspondents whom my father knew personally, plus a man on the *Tribune de Genève,* and offer them advance copies of the story. I was to start with the American agency because of the six-hour time difference between Geneva and their New York head office.

The writing materials presented no difficulty. I gave him a ballpoint pen I had in my handbag. Before I left I asked the nurse if he could have some magazines to read. While she was getting them I stole a packet of paper towels from a storage cabinet in the corridor.

My father hid the towels under his pillow.

"It'll be ready for you first thing in the morning," he said. "We'll show them what's what."

On the way out I met Michel.

"How did your father seem to you?" he asked.

"Very naturally annoyed," I said curtly, "and as sane, Doctor, as you are."

When we had spoken earlier he had been formal and rather stuffy. Now he surprised me by smiling. It was disarming. I suddenly found myself liking him.

"I'm sorry about the annoyance," he said; "I'll do my best not to add to it. Will you be in to see him again tomorrow?"

"In the morning if that's all right."

"About ten o'clock would be a good time." He hesitated. "May I make a suggestion?"

"About what, Doctor?"

"I'm sure you have many friends, but I think that, for the present anyway, it might be advisable not to discuss your father's statement with them."

"Because it sounds absurd, do you mean, or because it may be true?"

He smiled again. "I'd say those were both good reasons for discretion, wouldn't you?"

He did his best to warn me, you see, but I was still under my father's spell and didn't understand. I thought that he was trying to plant doubts in my mind, and for a moment I was on the point of telling him what I was really planning to do. Then I remembered that he was in a position to upset the plan if he wanted to, and I changed my mind. I merely said that I was very grateful to him for his advice and left without saying whether I meant to take it or not.

My father was looking much better when I saw him the following morning. He was still unshaven and the bruise looked horrible, but there was colour in his cheeks and his eyes were bright. The nurse said that he had had a good night.

The moment she was out of the room he brought out a folded wad of paper towels from under the bedclothes and thrust it into my hand.

"There it is," he said. "Go on, read it. Tell me what you think."

I unfolded the towels and read.

The story was headed "An Unholy Alliance" and there was a subtitle, *CIA's New Partner in Crime*.
It went on:

> The Central Intelligence Agency's deep devotion to the spirits of peaceful coexistence and international brotherhood is well known. It was inevitable, perhaps, that such devotion would lead them occasionally into strange and malodorous by-ways. Even so, the Congress and people of the United States, to say nothing of America's NATO allies, may well be sur-

prised to learn just how strange and malodorous some of those by-ways can be.

They will certainly be appalled.

In neutral Switzerland, of all places, the CIA has now allied itself with the notorious Soviet Committee of State Security, better known as the KGB, in a joint conspiracy of terror and coercion.

Incredible? One would have thought so. Impossible? One would have hoped so. Unfortunately, it is the squalid truth, and we have evidence to prove that it is.

There is no hearsay about our evidence. It is hard and incontrovertible. And for a very good reason. It is firsthand. The most recent victim of this iniquitous East-West gangster collaboration has been none other than the managing editor of Intercom—*this reporter—and his evidence comes to you direct from a hospital bed.*

Here are the ugly facts.

My father can make almost any "fact" ugly if he puts his mind to it, and he had uglified these with such gusto that I had difficulty recognizing some of them. The interview with Goodman and Rich in our apartment read like an account of a hatchet murder. While he didn't exactly say that we were both lying in pools of blood on the floor at the end of it, that was the impression he conveyed. His description of the session with Morin and Schneider at the Chateau Europa was, of course, horrendous. The attack in, and escape from, the office was a nightmare sequence out of an old German silent film. The car accident became an attempt to silence the voice of *Intercom* by murdering the editor. I couldn't help laughing.

He wasn't offended; he responded by quoting Shakespeare.

"But, since I am a dog, beware my fangs," he

said with a grim smile. "That'll shake them up, eh?"

"It will. But don't you think it may shake them the wrong way? Don't you think you ought to tone it down a bit?"

"This is no time to be pulling punches."

"But you do want to be believed."

He thought for a moment and then nodded. "You may have a point. Give it to me."

He began to edit it. After ten minutes he handed it back. The first part was unchanged, but the ugly facts had changed considerably. They were still ugly, but no longer unbelievably so. He had removed all the wilder adjectives and adverbs.

I put the paper towels in my bag and he gave me another one with the list of people I had to telephone written on it. I promised to return that evening and tell him what the reactions had been.

I must say that Nicole was very kind that day. She hadn't heard about the accident, of course, but as soon as I told her what had happened and explained about the new lead piece, she volunteered to go and open up the office and help with the typing. As a result I was able to start telephoning early in the afternoon.

The reaction of the American who was first on the list was fairly typical. After I had read the piece to him, there was a silence. Then he said: "Ted's got to be kidding."

"He isn't kidding."

"He's really going to print that?"

"It will go out Tuesday."

He sighed. "Okay, Miss Carter. Maybe they can use a laugh back home. I'll have the office send a messenger over for the copy." He started to say goodbye, then stopped. "By the way, Miss Carter, which hospital is your father in?"

I told him.

They were not all as easygoing as that, however.

My father had omitted some names from the ugly facts. For example, Goodman became "a thug masquerading as an American reporter," Madame Coursaux was referred to as "a French-speaking woman agent claiming to be a dealer in rare manuscripts" and Morin was "bullyboy Number Two." The Frenchman I spoke to wanted the names and was disbelieving when I said I didn't know them.

The German was even more difficult. He cross-examined me. My father's assertion that he was the *latest* victim of the CIA-KGB conspiracy, he said, clearly meant that he knew of earlier victims. Was he implying that Major General Horst Wendland, deputy chief of West German Intelligence, and Rear Admiral Hermann Luedke, NATO chief of staff for logistics in Belgium, had been among those early victims?

When I said that I had never heard of those persons, he became sarcastic. General Wendland's so-called suicide and the murder of Admiral Luedke, he informed me, had been widely publicised events. How could I not have heard of them? He, too, wanted to know which hospital my father was in.

So did the man on the *Tribune de Gèneve*.

It was six o'clock in the evening when I got back to the hospital.

Then I was told that I couldn't see my father. I must see Dr. Loriol.

I asked why and was told that those were Dr. Loriol's orders. No, there had been no change in my father's condition.

I asked to see Dr. Loriol. He wasn't available.

DR. MICHEL LORIOL
(written statement*)

My orders concerning Valerie were misinterpreted. The reason that I was not available was that I was with Commissaire Vauban in his office.

---

*Translated by C.L.

Earlier that afternoon I had been informed by the police duty officer that the briefcase from Monsieur Carter's car was now at the commissariat and that I could examine the contents there if I still wished to do so.

I went to the commissariat. After I had read the Arnold Bloch file, I telephoned Commissaire Vauban at his home and informed him that, in my opinion, the statements Monsieur Carter had made the previous day to the police, to the house surgeon and later to me had a factual basis. I suggested that they ought now to be treated seriously.

He said that he would leave at once for his office and asked me to wait there. As I was on call at the hospital, I telephoned to them to let them know that I would be delayed. I was informed that two journalists were there requesting interviews with Monsieur Carter.

I gave orders that no visitors, *with the exception of Mlle Carter,* were to be permitted to see her father. I added, however, that, if Mlle Carter did come to visit him that evening, I would like to see her first. To be candid, I was looking forward to giving her personally what seemed at that moment to be an encouraging piece of news. Unfortunately, some officious person at the hospital misrepresented my request by turning it into a prohibition.

When Commissaire Vauban arrived I reported on my interview with Monsieur Carter in detail and showed him the Bloch file. When he had read it he decided that he would himself take a statement in writing from the patient. He asked me if it could be taken at the hospital that night.

It would, I admit, have been much better if I had immediately agreed. The security service would have been alerted sooner and, although the news agencies already had Monsieur Carter's version of the story, he would at least have time to withdraw his own publication of it.

However, I did not immediately agree; I temporised. What I had in mind, of course, were the charges already pending against Valerie's father. I thought that by exaggerating slightly the gravity of his condition and recalling the mental strain to which he had been subjected, I might incline the Commissaire towards dropping the charges. I said that if it were absolutely essential to have the statement that night I would not object, but that I would prefer to wait. I spoke of delayed reactions. If the patient's condition was still unchanged the following day, I added, he would probably be permitted to leave the hospital and complete his recovery at home. It might be better, I said, to take his statement there.

Valerie and her father have said harsh things about Commissaire Vauban. They have been a little unjust, I think. He was genuinely concerned about his too-hasty dismissal of the earlier statements and anxious to retrieve his mistake. He was also considerate enough, in spite of his anxiety, to agree to wait until the following morning before taking the written statement. However, he did insist that it be taken before the patient was discharged from the hospital. That, I think, was not unreasonable under the circumstances. The failure at that point was mine. I should have agreed to his taking the statement that night, and I should have had the sense to tell him about the journalists who had been at the hospital seeking interviews. If I had done those things, Valerie's father might have been saved a great deal of embarrassment.

FROM THEODORE CARTER
(verbal communication)

"Embarrassment" for God's sake!

I was threatened with a two-year jail term and a fifty-thousand-franc fine. He calls *that* embarrassment?

I call it something else, Mr. L. However, I told you at the beginning that there were some things I still couldn't talk about, and I meant it. No, not even in confidence, not even off the record.

Look, there used to be a notice on one of the cages at the Paris Zoo. It became famous. You know the one I mean?

"This animal is vicious; when attacked, it defends itself."

That about sums up the attitude of the Swiss federal security boys. When I was attacked, I defended myself with the only weapons I know how to use—words—and their reaction was to chain me up and muzzle me.

Well, the chain may be off now, but the muzzle isn't. As long as I want to live and work in Switzerland, that's a fixture.

What you've had so far from me is a detailed, personal account of events that are, so to speak, in the public domain. I don't mean that you could have got it from anyone else; my voice is the only authoritative one; I mean that, as far as confidential stuff is concerned, that's the end of the line. If you're going to tread on the toes of the bogeymen, don't ask me to help you.

No, dammit, I'm not being overcautious. If you want to hear what my dear old pals Major X and Captain Y of Bureau H said and did, ask them yourself.

If I were you, though, I'd stick to guesswork, or narrative reconstruction, as you call it. It's safer.

Okay. On your own head be it, Mr. L. But don't say I didn't warn you.

NINE

NARRATIVE RECONSTRUCTION
December 19 to 23

Theodore Carter's refusal to run the risk of again incurring the displeasure of the Swiss counter-intelligence service was not unexpected; his indignation at having incurred it in the first place, however, is harder to understand. Few foreigners who have lived and worked in Switzerland, and certainly no foreign journalist living and working there, could be unaware of the Federal Republic's extreme sensitivity on the subject of espionage within its borders, nor of the reason for that sensitivity. Espionage activity, even when Swiss security is not threatened and no Swiss nationals are involved, is considered objectionable because it violates the Republic's neutrality.

It is certain that, for a time, Carter was seriously threatened with prosecution under Article 301 of the Swiss Criminal Code. This article states that any person "who carries on an information service for the benefit of one foreign state and to the detriment of another foreign state anywhere within the territory of the Federal Republic of Switzerland, or who recruits for such services or who assists them in any way," may be punished by imprisonment or a heavy fine. It was under Article 301 that Rudolf Rössler, that remarkable World War II spy who used the code name "Lucy," was tried in 1953. The prosecution held that, in acting contrary to the interests of the United States, Great Britain, France, West Germany and Denmark, through his work in Lucerne for Czech intelligence, he had violated Swiss neutrality.

Carter, of course, was never engaged in espionage activity of that kind, but he was certainly carrying on an information service within the meaning of Article 301; and, though the beneficiaries were not foreign states, those who suffered detriment were. No doubt he claimed that he had acted inadvertently and unintentionally, that he had been unaware of having committed an offence; and since he was never brought to trial, his explanations were evidently accepted in the end. But it must have been difficult to accept them. He admits himself that by the time he received the fourth bulletin, he already suspected that *Intercom* was being used to peddle secrets. In the light of that admission his indignation appears both unwarranted and disingenuous. The true basis for it, probably, was anger at his own folly. Having become involved in a conspiracy he did not understand, he had at first lost his head and then gone on to commit what he knew to be a monumental indiscretion.

The Swiss do not like being reminded that their country is one of the most spy-infested in the world; and, unless Swiss national security is directly involved, espionage cases are rarely reported at length. Spy scandals that would be given front-page coverage in other Western countries are mentioned briefly, if at all, on an inside page in Switzerland. The subject is distasteful there. Nothing could have been better calculated to prejudice the police and counter-intelligence investigators against Carter than the commotion he aroused in the international press. The investigators, used to working quietly and secretly behind security barriers, were suddenly exposed to the nagging importunities of foreign reporters and the glare of publicity.

They had other difficulties. Carter's wild allegations about a CIA-KGB terrorist plot had been taken seriously by one or two French and German newspapers with circulations in Switzerland. Diplomatic protests and denials were soon being bandied about. As a consequence, the investigators, too, were obliged to take the allegations seriously.

While it is easy to dismiss a story as nonsense on the grounds that it is against all reason, it is often quite hard to *prove* that it is nonsense; and, even when the proof is forthcoming, there will always be the credulous few who refuse to accept it. The trouble with Carter's story, of course, was that bits of it were true. He *had* had disturbing encounters with representatives of both the CIA and the KGB, and for reasons that had a common origin—the SESAME bulletins he had been publishing. It was perhaps inevitable that, in a moment of stress, a man with his kind of imagination should begin to suspect that the CIA and the KGB might be collaborating with each other. It was reckless of him, however, to broadcast his suspicion in terms that presented it as a demonstrable truth. The men from counterintelligence who questioned him assumed, naturally, that he knew more than he would admit to. As a result, it took them some time to disentangle the facts in his story from the embellishments.

His cooperation in the process was less than wholehearted. According to the Canadian consular official who was permitted to interview Carter in the police commissariat six days after the accident, he did not tell the investigators of his secret arrangement to publish the allegations about the CIA-KGB plot in *Intercom* until late Tuesday night. By then, of course, the December 20 issue was in the mails and out of reach.* He said nothing at all about the electret bulletin, which also appeared in

---

*Dr. Loriol's well-meaning supposition that earlier contact with the counterintelligence service would have changed his prospective father-in-law's mind about publication does more credit to his heart than to his head.

that issue, and when confronted with it he claimed airily that he had forgotten to take it out.

As we have seen, his indiscretion with the press had already antagonised the investigators. This further demonstration of his intransigence and irresponsible readiness to deceive certainly toughened their attitude towards him. The decision to arrest him, however, probably sprang as much from their determination to keep him away from the foreign reporters who were plaguing them as from the desire to teach him a lesson.

He was arrested on the Wednesday morning and arraigned in the afternoon. The judge ordered that he be held in custody for questioning. Bail was refused. The judge also granted warrants to search the *Intercom* offices and Carter's apartment.

Although Carter did not know it then, that day, Wednesday, December 21, was his last as the editor of *Intercom*.

Dr. Bruchner, too, has to be careful what he says about the *Intercom* scandal. However, some of the essential facts concerning the events of that week are matters of public record, and others can be deduced.

On Monday, December 19, Dr. Bruchner received a second offer from Bank Schwob for the shares of Intercom Publishing Enterprises A.G. This offer he transmitted to Arnold Bloch by telegram, using the Brussels *poste restante* address which he had been given three days earlier. The following day Bloch replied, also by telegram, accepting the offer and giving instructions for the payment of the purchase price. The instructions were that the money should be paid into a numbered account with the Bâle correspondent of a Lebanese bank.

Dr. Bruchner at once reported the acceptance of the offer to Bank Schwob.

No Bâle newspaper that morning had made any reference to the Carter imbroglio or to the events in Geneva; but in the late afternoon one of Dr. Bruchner's law partners drew his attention to a column in an American newspaper published in Paris. This particular paper had chosen to ridicule Carter's allegations, and the task of reporting them had been delegated to the staff humorist. He had gone to work with a will. General Novak's controversial career had been recalled in hilarious terms. *Intercom* was described as "the Batman of the funny-farm set" and its editor as "the Lone Ranger of the lunatic fringe." The allegations were dismissed by listing some of the more preposterous of *Intercom's* earlier excursions into "cloud-cuckoo land." It was an amusing and destructive piece of work.

Dr. Bruchner's response to it was curious.

It must be remembered that he had had a disturbing two days. The second offer from Bank Schwob had astounded him, and its acceptance had flustered him. He had managed to discuss the arrangements for payment and transfer with Dr. Schwob as if the transaction were a perfectly ordinary one; but it had been an effort to do so, and he had ended the conversation with the feeling that he had been imagining the whole thing.

The price that had been put on the *Intercom* shares was two million francs, almost half a million dollars. That had made Dr. Bruchner's head spin. What happened when he saw the column from Paris was that his head began to spin in the opposite direction. The man unable to believe the evidence of his senses was transformed suddenly into a man with a deal slipping through his fingers, a man selling a property valued at two million francs which has just been publicly labelled as worthless.

Dr. Bruchner called the *Intercom* office, spoke to Mlle Deladoey and learned that Carter was out of the hospital and apparently none the worse for his experiences. Thereafter, Dr. Bruchner forgot all about Carter and the allegations. He devoted the rest of his day to praying that neither Dr. Schwob nor his client read the English-language newspapers and to preparing the share transfer documents. He airmailed them to Brussels that night. If the deal was still on, he was determined that not a moment should be lost in consummating it.

Dr. Bruchner had some bad moments the following morning. Both the Radical Democratic and Independent newspapers carried pieces about *Intercom*. They said much the same thing. The Geneva police and the federal attorney general's office were investigating complaints made by Theodore Carter, editor of the *Intercom* newsletter, that he had been assaulted by representatives of certain foreign intelligence agencies and that those agencies were conspiring together to suppress the publication of news. One paper added noncommittally that Carter, a Canadian national, had recently been involved in a traffic accident in which he had suffered a head injury.

Dr. Bruchner was certain that, even if Dr. Schwob had not read these stories himself, someone in the bank would have drawn his attention to them; but at their meeting that day neither Dr. Schwob nor his procurator made any reference to Carter. The meeting was businesslike and brief. At the end of it a very relieved Dr. Bruchner left with a draft for two million francs, which he immediately paid into an escrow account. As soon as he received the signed share transfers from Bloch he would pay the money into the Lebanese bank, record the transaction in Zug and report back to Dr. Schwob. He expected then to learn the identity of the client for whom Bank Schwob was acting as nominee and, since he was still the sole director of the company, receive the new owner's instructions. He was looking forward to that moment.

The share transfers, signed by Bloch, arrived back in his office on Thursday. He delivered them personally to Dr. Schwob together with the share certificates. The transaction was completed.

"When," Dr. Bruchner asked, "may I expect to hear from the new proprietors?"

"I shall continue to act on their behalf," said Dr. Schwob. "My present instructions are that they plan a reorganisation of the company's affairs. As a first step in this reorganisation they wish to discontinue publication of the newsletter *Intercom*. They would like this decision to take effect immediately."

Dr. Bruchner was for a moment too bewildered to say anything. Dr. Schwob went on.

"The staff, including Carter, may be given two months' wages in lieu of notice. You should dispose of the lease of the Geneva offices as best you can and sell the contents. However, all *Intercom* records together with the mailing list—that is very important—and the Addressograph plates should be taken into your own custody and stored for the time being. You will receive further instructions about them later."

The only further instruction that Dr. Bruchner received was given three weeks later. It was to the effect that Intercom Publishing Enterprises A.G. should be placed in liquidation. No explanation was given. However, by then Dr. Bruchner had no need of an explanation. By then he had been interviewed by counterintelligence.

A great deal of nonsense is talked, and written, about Swiss banking secrecy. True, it is an offence punishable by fine or imprisonment for a Swiss bank employee to disclose a client's business; and he may be punished even for revealing the existence of an account without the owner's permission; but that secrecy is by no means inviolable. When there is reason to believe that it may be protecting a person who has committed a felony punishable under the Swiss Criminal Code, a court order may be obtained empowering a banker to disclose information.

It is virtually certain that, during the week following the share transfer, the counterintelligence investigators did apply for and obtain such an order; and it is no less certain that Dr. Schwob told the investigators the name of the purchaser of the *Intercom* shares.

Who was that purchaser?

Someone covering for a foreign intelligence service, undoubtedly; but for which service? And what type of cover did it employ?

Dr. Schwob's lips are again sealed, of course, but it is possible to draw some conclusions. No banker of Dr. Schwob's substance and reputation would act for a client in a negotiation of that kind unless he knew the client well and valued his normal business. Nor would he act for a client known to have connections with a foreign intelligence service. He must, therefore, have believed that there were valid commercial reasons for his client's costly determination to liquidate *Intercom*. Only a corporate client in the same line of business as Bloch's imaginary French and West German associates could have pretended convincingly to have such reasons. The case for concluding that a big company was used as cover for the operation is reinforced by the remark about "prudence" made by the banker when Bloch's price was made known to him. There is the hint of a threat in it. Men like Dr. Schwob do not threaten violence; however, they have been known to warn the ambitious against becoming too greedy and to remind adventurers that powerful corporations have the resources with which to punish bad faith. The instruction, given to Dr. Bruchner, to secure the *Intercom* mailing list and Addressograph plates shows the kind of bad faith Dr. Schwob's client had in mind. When *Intercom* died it was to stay dead. There was to be no rebirth under another name.

There are several Swiss-based corporations, owned predominantly by non-Swiss shareholders, with important arms and defence contracts. Some have their primary connections with NATO countries, but others do business (mainly in machine tools and chemicals) with the Soviet Union, East Germany, Romania and Hungary. Any one of them might have been used as the cover. The refusal of Swiss counterintelligence to give out any information on this subject was severely condemned in the left-wing West German press.

There has also been some criticism of the Swiss in NATO command circles. It has been said that, if the investigators had moved more energetically, the whole *Intercom* transaction could have been stopped and the true identity of Arnold Bloch established. Theodore Carter was first interrogated by counterintelligence on Tuesday, December 20, and arrested on the Wednesday. The *Intercom* office was searched the same day. Why, the critics ask, was Dr. Bruchner not told at once that *Intercom* was under investigation? He was at that time in touch with Bloch by mail and telegraph through the Brussels *poste restante* address. Why was that address not discovered earlier and given to the Belgian authorities in time for them to identify the user of it?

The complaint is as ill-informed as it is unfair. It must be remembered that what counterintelligence were investigating was the suspected violation on Swiss territory of a Swiss law designed to protect Swiss neutrality. Their primary concern was with Carter and with those elusive persons whom he accused of harassing him. The scene of the action was Geneva. Bloch was outside their jurisdiction. Drs. Schwob and Bruchner were doing nothing illegal, and no court would have stopped the share transfer from taking place. Carter had the Brussels address, it is true, but in the confusion he completely forgot about it.

On the night when he was attacked in his office, he had stuffed the telegram from Dr. Bruchner, the telegram giving him the address, into his overcoat pocket. A few minutes later he had been sick and in the process soiled the coat. In the hospital, on

Monday, his clothes were returned to him so that he could leave; but as soon as he got back to his apartment his daughter sent both his suit and the overcoat to the cleaners. The telegram went with the overcoat and was returned with it on Friday. Miss Carter immediately showed it to the investigators; but by that time it was useless. By then, Bloch had dissolved into thin air and the consortium's two million francs were on their way to Lebanon.

Admittedly, Colonel Jost and Colonel Brand were fortunate. If Carter had transferred the telegram from his overcoat pocket to his Bloch file, things might have happened a little differently—but only a little. As we shall see, Jost and Brand had planned with great care and ingenuity. After Wednesday, December 21, the day the two million went into Dr. Bruchner's escrow account, they ran no risk at all of failure. Their Christmas present was safe beneath the tree.

Who, then, was Santa Claus?

There are four prime suspects.

FROM THEODORE CARTER

At that point Latimer's manuscript ends.

According to Nicole Deladoey, he worked from notes made on cards which he kept in a small box. Presumably the names of the suspect companies were there. However, during the investigation following his disappearance the cards were all removed from his hotel room. They, too, have disappeared.

Intercom was silenced.

Charles Latimer was silenced.

Those who silenced them are themselves now mute.

Mine is the only voice left.

From Theodore Carter

OBIT AND ENVOY

1

The last person known for certain to have seen Charles Latimer alive was the Avis counter clerk at the airport to whom he delivered the key of his rented car. The time was just before noon.

A French passport inspector at the nearby frontier post on the road to Ferney-Voltaire reported seeing an elderly man answering Latimer's description. He had been travelling in a car with two other men, and the time had been about 12:30 P.M. However, the inspector could not be sure of the day. He had remembered the man, who had been carrying a United Kingdom passport, chiefly because he had been wearing very dark sunglasses. The inspector had asked the man to remove the glasses so that he could compare the photograph in the passport with the face of its holder. He had no special recollection of the other two men.

It was established that this particular inspector was unusually fussy about sunglasses and frequently asked travellers to remove them. His evidence was dismissed in the end as inconclusive; but it tended to confirm the cantonal police in their already well-founded belief that Latimer had left Switzerland alive and well, and of his own free will. Thereafter, their interest in his subsequent fate could only be academic; and, in the complete absence of further evidence of any kind about his movements after May 31, public interest also faded. When there are no developments to report, unsolved mysteries rarely stay long in the news.

Valerie said at one point that I admired and envied Latimer. I did indeed admire his work; it has given me many hours of pleasure. Perhaps I envied him, too; I certainly wish that I had known him better. I still find it hard to think of him as dead. Of the manner of his death I try not to think at all. My great regret is that, during the period immediately prior to his disappearance, our relations, which earlier had been more or less friendly, had become soured. My refusal to tell him about the security investigation had annoyed him, and I in turn had been piqued by his attempts to pump Valerie on the subject. She and Dr. Loriol dined with him once or twice; but, although I too had been invited, I didn't go.

It wasn't only pique that kept me away, though he probably thought it was. I was at that time beginning to build up my translation bureau. Using the apartment as an office with Nicole Deladoey as a part-time secretary had been all right at the beginning, but as the work began to grow it became necessary to make other arrangements. Nicole's going to work for Latimer precipitated the move. I hired a full-time girl to replace her and installed a mimeo machine. The people living in the apartment below soon complained about the noise, so a proper office became essential. I hadn't much time to spare for Latimer during those weeks.

The news of his disappearance disrupted everything. In spite of the cover-up job done by the security people, Latimer's connection with the *Intercom* affair and the fact that he had been at work on a book about it couldn't be hushed up. Paragraphs mentioning the forthcoming book had already appeared in American and British publishing journals.

We shall hear more about those paragraphs later. Almost certainly one or another of them triggered the disappearance. First, though, I must explain my own position.

The immediate effect on me of the disappearance was that for a few days I became news again. With no solid leads to go on, the reporters naturally dug around for some sort of angle on the story, and I was it. That was not only bad for my new business, it also brought me once again to the attention of the bogeymen and the police. But I had learned my lesson. I was extremely careful what I said, and mostly I said nothing. As I had hoped, the reporters became bored with me and it wasn't long before the police decided that I could be of no help to them in their efforts to trace Latimer. Nicole Deladoey knew, of course, that Latimer had been sending me a carbon of the first draft manuscript, chapter by chapter, for comment; but, even if it had occurred to her to mention the fact to the police, I doubt if she could have persuaded herself to soil her lips with my name. By the time I heard from the publishers about the revised first draft in her possession, I was, as far as the police were concerned, of no interest as a source of further information.

So, when I got hold of the revised draft and began to read between the lines I was able to keep what I saw there to myself.

I use the phrase "read between the lines" in a loose sense. In fact, it was the changes Latimer had made in his first draft that enabled me to get at the truth. Two of those changes were of major importance.

Chapter One, which had originally consisted of an exchange of letters between us, had been rewritten as a "narrative reconstruction" with some passages from the letters quoted to give the effect of dialogue. However, in one of those passages there was a significant deletion. In a letter to me he had written, "Through a friend *in the country where I spend the autumn of my days* I became acquainted with the man I am calling 'Colonel Jost' in the book."

The words that I have here italicised were deleted for the second draft.

Why?

His literary conscience could have been troubling him, of course. "The autumn of my days" is a pretty dreadful euphemism, and, although he had a weakness for mandarin adornment, he wasn't that dreadful a writer. But if the deletion had been decided upon for reasons of taste, why had he not replaced the euphemism with the information it had partly concealed? No reference to his age, coy or otherwise, had been in the least necessary. Why had he not said, "Through a friend in Majorca I became acquainted . . ." and so on?

The answer must be, I decided, that Colonel Jost was now living in Majorca and that Latimer had seen that even an oblique reference to the place in that passage would have given the game away.

The other deletion that especially interested me was more substantial. I had given him a detailed account of the meeting I had had in the *Intercom* offices with the man calling himself Werner Siepen. I had suggested that the man was really Colonel Jost and had carefully described him to Latimer. He had agreed that my description fitted the Colonel Jost he knew.

The whole of my account of the meeting and all later references to it had been cut out. And not just crossed out; eight pages of the typescript had actually been removed. Bridge sentences had been pencilled in on the pages preceding and following the cut.

My reactions to this cut were mixed. I was annoyed at first. I thought that he had cut those pages because they made him look less well informed than he had claimed to be. Then annoyance gave way to relief. For about half a minute I felt quite grateful to Latimer. He had seen, and I hadn't, that anyone *known* to be able to identify Colonel Jost might have a thin time with the bogeymen when the book was published.

That was the moment when my head began to clear, when I began to re-examine the whole picture that had been presented to me.

It looked, on the face of it, as if Latimer had made that cut to protect me; but how had he proposed to protect himself? By disappearing and leaving his book unfinished? Clearly not. How then?

As a distinguished scholar and a well-known writer he was probably in a position to cock a snook at the spooks and bogeymen. Moreover, he lived on a Spanish island, and Spain is not a member of NATO. Any revelations he might have had to make about the nominal purchaser of *Intercom* would no doubt have been answered with a bland denial, and any speculation about the intelligence agency which had financed the purchase would have been coldly ignored. Providing that he didn't make a wrong guess about the purchasing company and get sued for libel, he had nothing much to fear from those quarters.

With Jost and Brand, however, things would be very different. If they were identified they would be exposed in their own countries as traitors and in their country or countries of refuge as politically undesirable crooks. The consequences would be at best highly unpleasant. Latimer and his book represented an appalling danger to them. He had made no attempt to conceal the fact that he could identify Jost. It was more than likely, too, that he knew Jost's true nationality and probably Brand's as well. No doubt he had written his first narrative reconstruction in the belief that he had made it useless as an aid to positive identification. Most of the little circumstantial touches he had put in—for example, the casual mention of the fact that Jost came from a country with a coastline exposed to North Sea gales—were clearly red herrings. As defences against professional investigatory techniques, however, such story-teller's tricks would be hopelessly inadequate. There are only fifteen nation members of NATO and only eight of them were occupied by German forces during Hitler's war. For someone on the inside with access to security records and data-processing equipment, the task of identifying the two would not be difficult. The moment they discovered what Latimer was up to, Jost and Brand would have to do something to stop him, or at least try to.

Latimer himself had seemed unaware of that aspect of the situation. True, in a letter to me he had spoken of taking risks, but he had never referred to them in our discussions. His attitude towards the project had been like the attitude he had ascribed to his two colonels on the threshold of their conspiracy; he had been playing a rather amusing intellectual game of "let's pretend." I had assumed —reasonably, I think—that publication of the book would come as a big and disagreeable surprise to Jost and Brand; and, remembering what I had been through, I had looked forward to the moment. As far as I was concerned the bigger and more disagreeable the surprise the better. It had never occurred to me that Latimer might have neglected to take precautions against premature disclosure of the book's subject matter.

His game-playing approach to the material had also produced some strange inconsistencies. In one place he had described Jost and Brand as hard-headed, self-reliant and resourceful men "with the special skills needed for the successful conduct of clandestine operations" and habits of discretion that were instinctive. Yet, in another place, and in order to authenticate his narrative reconstruction, he had explained that Jost "liked to talk." If Jost had talked as freely as the reconstruction suggested he would appear to be one of the blabbermouths of all time and about as well suited to the successful conduct of clandestine operations as a skid-row alcoholic. If I had not had firsthand evidence of the existence of the Arnold Bloch conspiracy, I would

have been tempted to dismiss the narrative reconstruction entirely and to conclude that Latimer's
ability deal with fact had at last been overcome by
his talent as a purveyor of fiction. As things were I
could only treat it with reserve and remember that
its author had unaccountably and under strange
circumstances vanished.

Latimer had once described me as being in the
position of an innocent bystander caught in a bank
hold-up or that of the victim of a practical joke
perpetrated by strangers. Was it possible, I wondered, that he had without knowing strayed into
one of those positions himself?

Two months after the disappearance, his London
publisher came to see me. I discussed with him
some of the questions I have raised here. The out-
come of our discussion was that I received a commission to act in Latimer's absence (now assumed
to be enforced) as a kind of editorial salvage man,
to gather what further material I could and attempt
to tie up some of the loose ends. My first task
would be to go to Majorca and try to locate Colonel
Jost. In the event (thought to be unlikely) of my
succeeding, I was to make a cautious approach to
him and find out if he were prepared to be interviewed by me, or, if he were not, whether he would
be willing to make a statement for publication.

I flew to Majorca at the end of the first week in
August.

Latimer's house was on a hillside above a small
inlet town on the southeast coast of the island. The
town was flanked by steep pine-covered slopes ris-
ing from beaches of soft sand and was overpower-
ingly picturesque. At that time of the year it was
also very hot. Luckily I was able to get a room at
an inn with a pleasant outdoor dining terrace.

I took the room for a week. If Jost were living
in or near the town I thought that that would give
me time enough in which to find him; and if I
failed to find him in that time I could reasonably
conclude that he didn't live there. In the latter

event I would check the nearby towns and villages
—there were two villages and one other town within
a ten-kilometer radius—and if I still failed, that
would be that. I would go home.

I was neither pessimistic nor optimistic about
my chances. As a young reporter I learned that in
order to find and interview persons who don't want
to be found and interviewed you often need luck as
well as ingenuity and persistence. For luck you can
only hope. I was relying on the other things. True,
I knew neither the name Jost was using nor his
nationality, and I had to remember that either or
both could be assumed; but I did know what he
looked like and that he was a foreign resident. I
also had a possible lead. The man from London
had told me that the Majorcan couple employed
by Latimer as cook-housekeeper and gardener were
still in his house and, since Latimer had not then
been presumed dead, were still being paid by his
accountant in Palma. It was my intention to talk to
the couple and find out who in the neighbourhood
had been Latimer's friends and acquaintances. If
Jost was among them I felt sure that it wouldn't
take me long to track him down. I had decided to
go up to the house first thing in the morning.

I never went. There was no need to go.

I dined at nine-thirty. That is early by Spanish
standards and, since the Anglo-American tourist
invasion hasn't yet reached that particular town, I
had the terrace to myself for a while. It was a fine
Mediterranean night. The air was still, but it had
cooled off a little and the sounds of crickets and
the waves on the beach below were soothing. I ate
a mountainous paella and drank a bottle of white
wine. Around ten-thirty the terrace began to fill up
and I began to think of sleep. However, I didn't
immediately do anything about it. I was comfortable
where I was and I knew that my room would still
be hot and stuffy. I ordered a brandy.

And then Jost came in.

2

He looked about ten years younger than when I had last seen him. His face and arms were deeply tanned and the sun and sea had bleached his hair white. The bifocals were gone. He wore a blue linen beach shirt, denim slacks and espadrilles. He exuded good health, and though he still wore his regretful little smile there was something fat-cat about it now. With him was a girl young enough to be his daughter, but obviously not his daughter. She had long, light-brown hair, a Modigliani face and a lean, seductive little body. There was nothing incongruous about the pair of them. If she was the kind of girl who liked going to bed with older men, he was the kind of virile older man that kind of girl usually has in mind. Evidently Colonel Jost had found a better cure for boredom in retirement than talk and detective stories.

They were valued patrons. The innkeeper's wife herself showed them to their table, fussing over them and chattering as she took their order. I heard her pass it on to the kitchen.

"Crayfish," she said; "large portions for Señor Siepen and the Señora."

That name really startled me. No doubt my mention of it had startled Latimer when I had told him about Jost's visit to *Intercom*. It also explained something. That big cut in the manuscript had been made to protect not me but Colonel Jost.

He hadn't seen me and I was glad he hadn't. I needed time to think.

Werner Siepen of Hamburg was clearly a very well-established and well documented identity; Jost had probably been building it up for years. It suited him. The West German passport that went with the identity was doubtless impeccable, and in Majorca there would be few to notice that his German accent wasn't quite Hamburg and fewer still to care.

But it had been careless of him to use the Siepen identity in Geneva. As far as I was concerned he was blown. All I had to do now was to let him know it, but do so in such a way as to inform him at the same time that, if he was prepared to answer some questions, he had nothing to fear from me.

He still hadn't seen me. I sipped my brandy and wondered what would be the best approach. It wasn't, I knew, going to be easy. Blown he might be, but he was in a strong position. My weakness was that I still didn't know his true identity. Those who did know it, his former chiefs, had almost certainly concluded by now that their former Director of Defence Intelligence had been one half of the partnership known as Arnold Bloch. Clearly, they would not advertise that conclusion unless they were obliged to do so; politically the revelation would be horribly embarrassing. When the *Intercom* scandal broke, Colonel Jost had had a choice of two courses. Course One meant staying on the job and, if suspicions were aroused and awkward questions were asked, standing pat, denying everything and counting on being believed. Course Two meant clearing out ahead of the questions, leaving those with the red faces to draw their own conclusions, and becoming Werner Siepen.

Wisely, perhaps, he had chosen the second course. True, he had forfeited his pension and lost his good name; but who needed a colonel's pension when he had a million Swiss francs in the bank, and who cared about losing a good name when the loss remained on the secret list? There was not very much left to expose about Jost. All he really had to fear from me was inconvenience—the inconvenience of having to change his identity again and find another place to live.

He was pouring a glass of wine for the girl when he saw and recognised me. For a moment our eyes met, then he went on pouring. He didn't spill a drop. He was a cool one.

I considered going over to his table, then decided to wait and let him come to me. He would have to find out whether my presence there was coincidental or not, and it would be better to let him make the first move. Once he had made it, though, I would have to get a hook into him. Until he had realised that he would be better off if he came to terms with me, there was nothing to stop him taking the first plane to the mainland in the morning and simply avoiding me. Even if I could have kept track of him—a big if—I was in no position to go chasing all over Spain; the expense money wouldn't have run to that.

I had another brandy and watched them eat crayfish. They both had hearty appetites. To pass the time I tried working myself up into a rage about them—or him anyway. Jost–Siepen had, after all, been instrumental in giving me a bad time—one of the worst I had known—and he had done so simply in order to have money in the bank and be able to sit on a terrace with a sexy girl friend and stuff his belly with crayfish. And I wasn't the only casualty now of that game for two players. Latimer, too, had been carried off the field. The nature and extent of his injuries were yet to be ascertained, but it was unlikely that they had been superficial. And here was Jost–Siepen, one of the winners, living it up like a bloody lord and . . .

But it was no good. I couldn't get angry. The only emotion of which I was capable just then— if it is an emotion—was curiosity. I badly wanted to know.

Eventually, Siepen called for the bill and they got up to go. As they did so I saw him say something to the girl and motion with his head in my direction. She smiled and then with a casual glance at me left the terrace. Colonel Jost, as I shall call him now, came over to my table. I stood up.

"We've met before, I think," he said in Spanish. "Señor Carter, isn't it?"

Spanish is not one of my languages. I knew he spoke English, so I answered him in it.

"Yes. We met in Geneva, Colonel."

His eyes flickered at the word "colonel," but he was still smiling.

"My name is Siepen."

"Yes," I said, "I remember. But we have mutual friends, Colonel, who know you better than I do."

"Do we?" His eyes were very watchful now.

"Charles Latimer, who was your neighbour here."

"Ah yes. And you were a friend of his?"

"I knew Arnold Bloch of Munich better, Colonel. In fact it was he who suggested that I should come here and see you."

He took that blatant lie calmly. "About a money matter, perhaps?"

"About a matter of information. He said you had some to sell."

"What price did you have in mind, Mr. Carter?" He spoke very quietly now.

"Anonymity, Colonel," I said. "Your privacy here."

He pursed his lips, then nodded. "I see no reason why we should not at least discuss the matter. Tomorrow perhaps? Or the next day?"

"Either would do." He made a movement as if to leave and I went on quickly. "Colonel, when we last met you gave me some advice. The man of sense, you said, submits to pressure with good grace. If for any reason you should not be available tomorrow or the next day, if, for example, you were suddenly to be called away on business, I

198

would have to conclude that anonymity and privacy were of no value to you."

He shrugged. "Privacy is of value to every man of sense. My car is outside and a lady is waiting. Join us if you wish."

His coolness was disconcerting. "Now?"

"Why not, if your business is so urgent?" He turned and started to walk out. I caught up with him at the kitchen door.

"Just a moment, Colonel," I said. "Where exactly are we going?"

He stopped and gave me an amused look. "Don't worry, Mr. Carter. You'll get back safely." He put his head inside the kitchen and called to the innkeeper's wife. "Señor Carter is an old friend. He is coming with me to my house to join me in a glass. Don't lock him out, Señora."

She came out, beaming, to assure him that she wouldn't. I received a look of approval. As a friend of Señor Siepen I had clearly gone up in her estimation.

The car was a B.M.W. and the girl was sitting at the wheel. Jost introduced me to her as he got in beside her. "This, *mein Schatz,* is Herr Carter. He is a friend of Herr Lewison and we have a little business to discuss. It won't take long." He patted her thigh.

He did not tell me his "treasure's" name. As I climbed into the back she gave me a quick smile and then started the engine.

Jost's house was on the other side of the inlet at the end of a hillside road crisscrossed by low-voltage power lines. He spoke only once on the way. We were passing a heavy wooden gate at the entrance to a driveway.

"Lewison's house," he said. "Have you been there?"

"No."

"A very nice property. It has a lemon grove." His own place was among fig trees and looked

199

like a remodelled farmhouse. The living room—the only room I saw—was furnished in a Spanish provincial style with upholstered chairs and sofas added for comfort. There was a large fireplace. A paved terrace had been added on the side facing the sea and vines were being trained over a rustic pergola to give shade from the sun. From the terrace a steep path led down to the beach some distance below.

When we reached the terrace Jost lit some candles mounted in wrought-iron brackets and then turned to me.

"Brandy or Scotch whisky?" he asked.

"Brandy, please."

The girl went back inside the house and presently an old maidservant brought us a bottle and some glasses on a tray.

Jost had motioned me to a chair, but he made no attempt at small talk. Neither did I. He lit one of his panatellas and we sat there in silence until the old woman had gone. Then he poured two drinks and pushed one towards me.

"Let us understand one another," he said. "We met once, briefly, when I purchased a subscription to a publication you edited. We have a mutual acquaintance, a writer named Lewison or Latimer, who seems to have disappeared from the face of the earth. That is the extent of our connection. I know nothing of this Arnold Bloch of whom you spoke. If you choose to ask hypothetical questions, my answers will be equally hypothetical. If you care to believe them, that is your affair. Do I make myself clear?"

"Quite clear, Colonel. You know nothing, you admit nothing."

He blew a cloud of smoke and eyed me through it. "Addressing me as Colonel, Mr. Carter, will get you nowhere," he said; "and if you think that that sort of knowingness impresses me, you are very much mistaken."

"It wasn't intended to impress you," I said untruthfully. "Since this is a hypothetical discussion, I assumed that a hypothetical courtesy would be in order. In his last book, the book I am now employed by his publishers to complete, Latimer said that you were a colonel. I accepted that. If he was wrong, of course . . ."

He flicked the subject away with his cigar ash. "It is unimportant."

"He also wrote that you liked to talk."

His mouth hardened. "I know only too well what he wrote."

"You've read his manuscript then?"

"Part of it, yes."

"He gave it to you to read?"

"No, Mr. Carter, he did not. When it was learned that he was writing a book on the subject of what the newspapers called 'the *Intercom* affair,' an interested party decided to take a look at the contents."

"Without Latimer's knowledge?"

"Naturally."

"Was the interested party you or Colonel Brand?"

"I know no one of that name." He shrugged. "Let us say it was Brand."

"And he passed it on. I see. It must have come as an unpleasant shock to both of you."

He took a sip of brandy and gave me a sombre look. "Mr. Latimer was a very clever man," he said; "he was also, I regret to say, completely irresponsible. Because of those things he wrote I was accused of betraying a valued friend."

"You mean you *didn't* tell Latimer the things he says you told him?"

"Of course I didn't. What do you take me for?" He was indignant now and jabbed the air with his cigar as he went on. "Because I thought I liked him, I told him a few stories, anecdotes about intelligence work. I knew he'd been in British intelligence during the war, an adviser in SOE or some such thing. We would sometimes—how do you say it?—swap yarns. And then one day I told him about the Mexican forger. That was the only mistake I made."

"But there was nothing secret about that story," I said. "It was reported. There are published accounts of it. It is common knowledge."

"It is, now. But he hadn't heard of it and *I* told him, and I used the phrase 'nuisance value.' One afternoon a few days later he came to me and began talking about the *Intercom* affair."

"You mean he'd put two and two together?"

Jost dropped his cigar on the stone paving and ground it out with his heel. "He had made one or two shrewd guesses," he said bitterly. "Like a cheap fortune-teller. Of course he told it to me as a story that he'd invented. It was a great joke for him. At times he could scarcely get the words out for laughing. He had even found out the date I bought this property and added that to the indictment."

There was nothing hypothetical about the discussion now. He was reliving that afternoon.

"What did you do, Colonel?"

"What could I do? I, too, treated it as a joke. What else could I have done?"

"You didn't deny it?"

"Of course not. I told you. It *had* to be treated as a joke and shared as one. Most of it *was* a joke—pure rubbish."

"Except for the dangerous bits he'd guessed right about. I see."

He frowned. "I couldn't be sure, you see, what he really believed. Did he believe the story itself or only that he had invented it? I thought that if I shared the joke he would become tired of it."

"But he didn't. Why do you call him irresponsible, Colonel?"

He bristled. "To distort a man's idle confidences and then use the distortions against him without his knowledge—you call that responsible? Or honourable?"

I felt like saying that Arnold Bloch could answer that question better than I, but refrained. I was there to listen, not score debating points.

"When he went away," Jost went on, "I was at first relieved. It meant that I no longer had to see him and listen to his nonsense. Then I heard that he was working in Switzerland and became anxious. Not on my own account so much as on Brand's. He is a sick man, you know, and still in his own country. He also has a family there."

"How did Latimer know that Brand had a kidney disease?" I asked. "You must have told him that."

He shook his head impatiently. "I once told him about a clandestine meeting with a colleague who had been to Evian to consult a kidney specialist. That's all. *I* didn't identify the colleague. Latimer did." He pushed the brandy bottle towards me and motioned to me to help myself. "That was one of his most dangerous guesses."

"Perhaps you told him more than you realised," I said. "After all, Colonel, you'd kept it all bottled up a long time. They say that the unconscious can play strange tricks on a man."

He looked at me with distaste. "Psychological mumbo-jumbo has never impressed me, Mr. Carter. Latimer was shrewd, I grant you, and I should have known better than to tell him about the Mexican forger. I've admitted that. It put the idea into his head. But all the rest was guesswork on his part." He took out a fresh cigar and pointed it at me. "Guesswork, pure and simple."

"Don't forget," I said, "that he'd read about the *Intercom* affair in the newspapers. When you see two pieces of a jigsaw puzzle that may fit, you put them together. If they do fit, you start looking for the other pieces nearby. That's not guesswork."

"Call it what you like. That fairy story of his was dangerous—dangerous for Brand anyway."

"What did you do about Brand?"

"I wrote alerting him to the situation."

"Using a French ten-franc note?"

He ignored that. "He wrote back sending me a clipping from some magazine, a booksellers' guide. It was about the book Latimer was writing. Brand wanted to know if I knew Latimer. I told him I did." He paused. "And then he wrote me this letter accusing me of betraying him. I made allowances, of course. A sick man . . ." He broke off with a shrug and reached for his matches.

"What happened to Latimer?" I asked.

He took his time lighting the cigar. "I don't know," he said finally; "I can only speculate. As I said, Brand was a sick man and no longer able to think clearly. He believed that it was possible to silence Latimer by—" he made little circular motions with the spent match—"by disposing of him. I warned him that that was not the way, that there would be records inaccessible to us, documents left behind, other persons involved. I was right, or you would not be here. I proposed instead that we should approach him, separately or together, and reason with him, persuade, pay him off if necessary."

"You wouldn't have succeeded in paying him off."

"Perhaps not. But we might have persuaded him to eliminate the dangerous material. However, Brand no longer trusted me. He wouldn't listen. He said that he was more vulnerable than I was and would make his own decisions. I tried to argue with him, but by then it was too late."

"What happened to Latimer?" I asked again.

He poured himself another drink. "I would guess that Brand wrote to Latimer in Geneva saying that he was willing to meet with him if Latimer was interested in further material for his book. But the meeting would have to be in a place of Brand's choosing and under conditions of extreme secrecy.

He probably gave him that cover story about the NATO interview in Evere along with other instructions." He smiled grimly. "I am sure that Latimer enjoyed participating for once in a little of what he chose to call 'this cloak-and-dagger foolishness.' "

"What kind of other instructions?"

"You know Cointrin airport. That new arrival-and-departure building is a big place. Until you have handed in your ticket and gone through passport control no one checks or controls your movements. Once Latimer had delivered the key of his car and walked away from the Avis counter he was as good as lost. Brand probably told him to go through the building and out to one of the other car parks where there would be someone waiting to drive him to a meeting place in France."

"You think he was taken via Ferney-Voltaire? There is, as you may know, some evidence that he was seen there."

"I think it probable."

"And then what?"

"I don't know."

"But you can speculate."

He sighed. "I have speculated a great deal. I will tell you what I believe. It can make no difference now. Brand is very ill. By the time this book of yours and Latimer's is published he will be dead."

He was silent for a moment. I waited.

"When it comes to killing," he went on slowly, "every man is a specialist. The one who can use a knife will always prefer it to a pistol. The poisoner never strangles, and the strangler does not carry a bludgeon. In time of war, when there is a wider choice of weapons and the killing is legal, it is the same. The combat soldier favours the weapon that best suits his temperament; the field commander tends to employ the arms and tactics that best suit his, usually those with which he has had an earlier success. Brand was no exception to the rule. He always thought tactically in terms of ambush and burial."

"Burial?"

"Brand," he said, "was trained originally as an engineer officer. He knew a great deal about the use of dynamite and high explosives. Quite early in the German occupation he succeeded in burying some enemy supply trucks by dynamiting a hillside above them. The terrain he fought over was suitable for that kind of operation and he was able to repeat that first success a number of times. On one occasion he derailed and partly buried a train by dynamiting a cutting. When he spoke of the need to deal with an opponent, he never spoke of defeating him but always of digging his grave."

"It's a common enough figure of speech."

He shook his head. "With Brand it wasn't just a figure of speech. That was the way he thought. I should know. Once, a few years ago, when we were driving together from Brussels to Cologne, we were held up on the road by some construction work. They were building a crossing for a new autoroute, and we saw them pouring concrete to make one of the supports. The caisson went deep into the earth and there was a big cage of steel reinforcing rods. We stopped to watch. It was an impressive thing to see the concrete pouring in—tons and tons of it. Brand was fascinated. When we moved on he said something I afterwards remembered. 'If I ever wished to dispose of an unwanted person I would have him taken to a construction site.'" He gave me a meaning look. "I have thought about that more than once since Latimer disappeared. Between Ferney-Voltaire and Strasbourg there must be many construction sites, I would say, and many deep graves ready to be filled."

I said nothing; I was feeling rather sick.

I must have looked it, too. He made clucking sounds. "Don't worry about it, Mr. Carter. Brand was never a barbarian. He would use experienced operatives. However it was done, I am sure that it was done quickly and that Latimer suffered no pain."

The girl came out of the house wearing a towelling beach jacket and carrying a flashlight. She announced that she was going for a swim.

Jost reached out a hand as she went by and caught her by the sleeve of the jacket. From the way she held the front of it I guessed that that was all she was wearing.

"I'll be down in a few minutes, my treasure," he said. "On this fine night I am sure that Herr Carter will not mind walking back to the inn."

"Not in the least," I said, and I meant it. I couldn't have taken much more of Colonel Jost. But there were still questions I had to ask.

When the girl had gone I said: "Why did you involve Skriabin in that bulletin about the seismograph? Was that Brand digging *his* grave?"

He chuckled. "Oh, that was my idea. Skriabin was the KGB *residentura* in Oslo and he had become a source of great irritation to our Norwegian friends. It occurred to me that a public embarrassment might quieten him down a bit. It did. His masters transferred him to Syria. They must have been quite annoyed."

"They were," I said. "I should know. They worked off some of their annoyance on me."

His eyes widened. "Surely, Mr. Carter, you are not complaining." He spread out his hands in the gesture of benediction I had seen once before. "Think how much you have benefitted from our association."

"Benefitted!" I had the last of my brandy in my throat and I choked on it.

"Certainly." He leaned forward and tapped my knee. "You are a different man from the one I met a year ago. Then you were tired and contemptuous of the work you did. You disliked yourself. Now, I detect a new confidence in you. Think. You are engaged in completing a book for the late, respected and much lamented Mr. Latimer. Would his publishers have employed the man you were a year ago? I doubt it. You have come to terms with yourself. If you are wise and take care of your health, happier years may lie ahead of you, a whole new future."

"Or to put it another way," I said sourly, "watch your step, Carter, and don't try double-crossing me. If my anonymity and privacy are threatened by anything you write, you and your future will find a grave like Latimer's. Is that the message, Colonel?"

He stood up, his smile firmly in place. "I'm glad we understand one another. Before you go, perhaps you will satisfy my own curiosity on one point. Did Latimer ever find out who it was who bought our shares?"

"He had a short list of four companies whom he suspected of having acted as agents for the real buyers. However, Swiss security impounded his records, so I don't know the names. Who, in fact, were the buyers?"

The smile became pained. "My dear Mr. Carter, I was hoping that you could tell me. Brand thought it must have been the KGB. My belief is that it was the BfV using CIA funds. But I don't *know*. It is most annoying."

"Why!" I asked. "You have the money. What does it matter now where it came from?"

He looked surprised. "Naturally it matters. The operation was ours, Brand's and mine. We planned it and we executed it. It was superbly successful. Not to know exactly *how* it succeeded, not to have all the information in one's hands, is intolerable. I shall find out eventually, of course. These things can't be hushed up indefinitely. Sooner or later somebody talks."

As we went through to the front door he suddenly gave a snort of amusement. "You know," he said, "for all his shrewdness, Latimer had his blind spots. He was completely wrong about one thing— completely and utterly wrong. Neither Brand nor I was ever in the least bit arrogant. Ambitious, yes, but never arrogant."

Once past the gateway to Latimer's villa I enjoyed the walk back to the inn.

ABOUT THE AUTHOR

ERIC AMBLER was born in London in 1909. Following his graduation from London University, he served an apprenticeship in engineering, toured England in a vaudeville act, wrote songs and, for several years, advertising copy. In the period from 1937 to 1940 Mr. Ambler won fame with five novels of intrigue which have become classics: *Background to Danger, Epitaph for a Spy, Cause for Alarm, A Coffin for Dimitrios* and *Journey into Fear.* He joined the British Army in 1940 and was discharged a lieutenant colonel in 1946, having been in charge of all military training, morale and education films for the Army. After the war, Mr. Ambler wrote and produced a number of motion pictures for the J. Arthur Rank Organization. For his screenplay of Nicholas Monsarrat's *The Cruel Sea* he was nominated for an Academy Award. In 1951, *Judgment on Deltchev*, his first novel in eleven years, was published. This was followed by *The Schirmer Inheritance* (1953), *State of Siege* (1956), *Passage of Arms* (1960), *The Light of Day* (1963), *A Kind of Anger* (1964) and *Dirty Story* (1967). Mr. Ambler is also the editor of *To Catch a Spy: An Anthology of Favorite Spy Stories* (1965).